W9-BLD-963

"Mommyhood at its comic and chaotic best!"

—RAY BLACKSTON, author of *Flabbergasted*

"Some novels make you plunge the depths of your heart in examination. Others make you examine your underwear drawer in frustration. Kimberly Stuart's *Bottom Line* does both! Delightfully funny, affirming, and full of characters so cool, this one is a keeper."

—CLAUDIA MAIR BURNEY,
author of the Amanda Bell Brown Mysteries

"A laugh-out-loud look at the perils and blessings of motherhood, *Bottom Line* is fresh and heartfelt. What a great read!"

—ANNE DAYTON and MAY VANDERBILT,
authors of *Emily Ever After* and *Consider Lily*

Also by Kimberly Stuart:
Balancing Act: A Heidi Elliott Novel, Book 1

BOTTOM LINE

Kimberly Stuart

A Heidi Elliott Novel
Book 2

NAVPRESS®

BRINGING TRUTH TO LIFE

OUR GUARANTEE TO YOU

We believe so strongly in the message of our books that we are making this quality guarantee to you. If for any reason you are disappointed with the content of this book, return the title page to us with your name and address and we will refund to you the list price of the book. To help us serve you better, please briefly describe why you were disappointed. Mail your refund request to: NavPress, P.O. Box 35002, Colorado Springs, CO 80935.

NavPress
P.O. Box 35001
Colorado Springs, Colorado 80935

© 2007 by Kimberly Ann Ruisch Welge

All rights reserved. No part of this publication may be reproduced in any form without written permission from NavPress, P.O. Box 35001, Colorado Springs, CO 80935. www.navpress.com

NAVPRESS, BRINGING TRUTH TO LIFE, and the NAVPRESS logo are registered trademarks of NavPress. Absence of ® in connection with marks of NavPress or other parties does not indicate an absence of registration of those marks.

ISBN-13: 978-1-60006-077-9
ISBN-10: 1-60006-077-3

Cover design by The DesignWorks Group, Tim Green, www.thedesignworksgroup.com
Cover photo of woman by Getty Images
Cover photo of girl by Getty Images
Author photo by Mindy Myers

Creative Team: Jeff Gerke, Jamie Chavez, Kathy Mosier, Arvid Wallen, Kathy Guist

This novel is a work of fiction. Names, characters, places, and incidents are either the product of the author's imagination or are used fictitiously. Any resemblance to actual events, locales, organizations, or persons, living or dead, is entirely coincidental and beyond the intent of either the author or publisher.

Stuart, Kimberly, 1975-
  Bottom line / Kimberly Stuart.
    p. cm. -- (A Heidi Elliott novel ; bk. 2)
  ISBN-13: 978-1-60006-077-9
  ISBN-10: 1-60006-077-3
  1. Stay-at-home mothers--Fiction. 2. Part-time employment--Fiction.
3. Lingerie--Fiction. I. Title.
PS3619.T832B68 2007
813'.6--dc22
                                    2006102323

Printed in the United States of America

1 2 3 4 5 6 7 8 9 10 / 11 10 09 08 07

FOR A FREE CATALOG OF NAVPRESS BOOKS & BIBLE STUDIES,
CALL 1-800-366-7788 (USA) OR 1-800-839-4769 (CANADA)

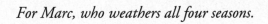

For Marc, who weathers all four seasons.

acknowledgments

I would like to extend my gratitude to . . .

. . . God, who seems to delight in showering mercy on ragamuffins like me.

. . . the kind people at NavPress, particularly Terry Behimer, Andrea Christian, Kate Berry, Jeff Gerke, Kris Wallen, and Kathy Mosier. Thanks to each of you for making this a better book.

. . . the fantastic Jamie Chavez, a fellow bibliophile who whipped this puppy into shape and did so with panache and a healthy dose of gut laughter.

. . . my gaggle of prereaders: Patti Ruisch, Jennifer Ruisch, Betsy Beach, and Stacie Stanley. Thank you for your diligence, your friendship, and your willingness to be honest with me, even if it meant you'd get smaller Christmas presents.

. . . Ginger Garrett and Claudia Mair Burney for rollicking laughter and steadfast friendship.

. . . my writers' group, Wendy, Jen, Kali, Dawn, and Mia, for the care and attention you brought to the editing table.

. . . Ashley Brandon, Tracey Orman, and Grandma Patti for loving my children to pieces. This book would have ended at brochure stage without you three.

. . . my legion of family and friends who assume I can do it.

. . . Ana, Mitch, and Marc, who love me still.

prologue

In the days before Nora, I had a job that paid in American dollars. I had a pension plan and benefits. I had regular interaction with all kinds of people who knew how to cut their own meat.

But then, in a heady moment of parental love, I decided to be a stay-at-home mom.

Now, I can just hear the applause of Phyllis Schlafly, Dr. Phil, Oprah. Namely, *all people who don't stay home.* And I'm not saying they are wrong to put the hope of America in the hands of mothers. I'm sure what I do is very noble. The stay-at-home mom raises children who will change the world! She is a warrior! A freedom fighter! A revolutionary!

But to be honest, there are days when I would trade all the Play-Doh in the world for one quiet pedicure and a hefty Christmas bonus. In American dollars, of course.

chapter/one

"Lovely."

"You think so?"

"You'll be the fairest of them all."

"That's quite the compliment." I squeezed my eyelids tighter to protect my corneas from jabs of purple eye shadow. "Can I look yet?"

"Not yet, silly. You need lipshtick."

"Lipshtick. Of course." I opened my eyes and puckered up.

My nearly four-year-old daughter, Nora, stood before me, face centimeters from my own. A flock of black eyelashes, expertly emphasized with Max Factor, framed wide blue eyes. A tiara struck a precarious balance on her crown of thick brown curls. She stuck her tongue out in concentration and drew a wobbly line of Chinese red near my lips, catching a few teeth en route. Stepping back to view her work, she sighed with pleasure. "All done."

"Fantastic," I said, rising from the footstool on which I sat. I held out my hand, bowed deeply. "Shall we?"

Nora smiled, scrambled to her feet. She pulled herself up to her full three feet of height and tilted her chin to an orator's pose. "The pumpkin car is waiting."

"Awesome," I said and took her hand.

She stopped, looked up with reproach. "Mommy, you're the prince." She had a touch of purple shadow, a sprinkling of blush and clear lip gloss. Such are the advantages when your makeup is done by someone with fine motor skills. "*I'm* the princess and *you're* the prince. You have to talk like a boy."

I looked down at my getup. Yards of white satin stuck out in a triangle starting at my waist. My wedding dress had experienced a renaissance as a result of Nora's princess fixation. I'd made the mistake of showing my daughter our wedding album and had been forced to reveal the sacred dress with the best twirling radius in the house. Nora didn't seem to mind that I couldn't zip up the back. Exposed skin didn't bother her as long as it didn't affect my ability to spin on demand.

I cleared my throat and lowered my voice. "Fine, my lady. I am your prince, as long as my dress doesn't cause any confusion."

Nora ignored me completely. She was practicing her own moves in a cheap princess imitation I'd found at Target. A better mother might have sewn a frilly play gown, or at least tried for vintage glamour from The Salvation Army. I'd shunned home ec in high school, had precious little time for thrift store digging, and was not a better mother.

"Prince?" Nora asked.

"Yes?" I replied.

Nora stopped spinning, hand on hip.

I cleared my throat and switched to baritone. "Sorry. Yes?"

"Where's the palace?"

What? Our cluttered house that hasn't been dusted since

'03 doesn't strike you as a fitting place for a ball?

My chance for retort was curtailed by the ringing doorbell. I swished toward the entryway, pulling a ratty cardigan around my shoulders to hide the gap in back. I peeked through the cut-glass window in our front door. The mailman waited with a stack of mail and an electronic clipboard. I pulled the door open and tried to avoid eye contact. I couldn't really move my eyelids due to the weight of purple caking, so this wasn't too difficult.

He smirked and showed me where to sign.

I scribbled in silence, then exchanged the clipboard for a certified letter and a stack of bills.

"Nice outfit," he said, ripping off a receipt.

"Thank you." I swished backward and curtsied as I closed the door.

℮ ℈ ℮

"MommyMommyMommy!"

"Coming." I left the bills on the table and returned to the ball. Nora was hopping by the couch, alternating feet.

"Mommy, I need to go potty."

"Okay. Call me if you need help."

"I *do* need help. With my dress." She was scurrying toward the bathroom while trying to keep her knees together.

I followed her and reached around to gather the tulle as she yanked down her underwear.

"I can't! I can't!" Nora's eyes filled with panic. In the not-so-distant past, wearing the contents of an emptied bladder wouldn't have raised a little eyebrow, but now the idea of wet pants made Nora shiver with disgust. I hurried to help her bare all.

I scooped her up and sat her tush on the toilet seat, bunching pink layers in my hand to keep them from the bowl below.

Nora sighed and let her head fall into her hands. "Made it."

"Next time let me know a little earlier and we'll have plenty of time."

"Mom," she said, voice muffled, "you're the prince."

☙ ✺ ☙

An hour later I threw a sixth Chinese-red cotton ball into the bathroom trash can. The voice of Mister Rogers as Lady Aberlin droned from the living room, where Nora sat in her dress munching handfuls of Goldfish. I had forty-five minutes to cast off my princely role and return to that of June Cleaver, casserole in hand, when my husband, Jake, returned from work.

I looked at my reflection in the bathroom mirror. My green eyes were still combating stubborn purple film, but that was a good distraction from the wrinkles that had started to surface. At thirty-two, I felt younger than I looked. After removing evidence left by the deft hands of Madame Nora, Makeup Artiste, I looked my age in dog years. I ran my fingers through my shoulder-length honey brown hair. Nora got her curls from me, I hated to say. I'd battled them all my life, enduring hours of straightening treatments and spending embarrassing amounts of money on flatirons. My current lifestyle, however, prohibited lengthy grooming rituals, so I was trying to embrace my curly self. Judging from today's look, I had a long way to go.

Much to my daughter's chagrin, my everyday wardrobe wasn't very regal. I tossed my wedding dress onto the bed and picked up worn jeans and a striped orange and blue T-shirt. Pulling my arms through the sleeve holes, I vaguely recalled a time when I would dress for the workday. In another life, I'd taught Spanish at Springdale High School on the south side of town. Those were days of skirts, hose, and sensible pumps. Now I was content with variations on a comfortable theme: jeans, shirts, and all forms of sweatshirts. On wild and crazy winter days I donned a sweater, and Jake could convince me to dress up on date nights, but as a rule, I was happy to donate my work clothes to those less fortunate rat-racers.

I tiptoed past the family room and into the kitchen, dodging the creaky boards in our hardwood. My passage unheeded by the Goldfish eater, I opened the fridge and took out broccoli, mushrooms, gingerroot, and strips of beef sirloin. Stir-fry tonight, per Jake's request. I'd even marinated the meat. I'd never learned to sew, but cooking hadn't been as elusive. Nobody would ever confuse me with Twiggy, but there was something to be said about dying fat and happy. Smug with a rare moment of organization, I dragged our wok out of the pantry and set it on the stove top. Broccoli rinsed and mushrooms brushed, I set the cutting board before me.

"Mommy, will you color with me?" Nora stood in the doorway to the kitchen, blue and green marker streaking the front of her dress, bodice to hem. Another reason I shopped at Target. She held a fistful of uncapped markers in one hand.

An open coloring book was sandwiched between her elbow and hip.

"I have to cook dinner, sweetie." I peeled off two cloves of garlic from the bulb.

"Pleeeease?" Nora asked. Two markers dropped on the floor. "Ten minutes?"

I looked at her rainbowed face and wanted to kiss the Crayola genius who'd developed washable technology. "Five minutes."

"Six."

"Five." I followed Nora to the kitchen table and helped her spread out the supplies. "What are we going to color?"

"This one." She pointed to the open page. A toothy giant loomed above a frightened Jack standing by the beanstalk.

"Really?" I asked, unsure. "He looks like he's not very nice."

"Yes, he is," Nora said, coloring the giant's teeth in bold brown strokes. "He's a nice giant. Jack is happy to see him."

Is that why Jack is sweating and trying to run off the page? I started coloring the beanstalk orange. The green was being used for Jack's hair. "What happened to your Noah's Ark coloring book?" A parade of paired-off animals seemed more cheerful, at least until the rain began to fall.

"I think it's in Daddy's car."

I doubted it. Somewhere along the way, our daughter had heard this excuse for a missing item and had taken to ascribing car blame when household objects disappeared.

"We'll have to check when he gets home from work."

"Let's go see Daddy at his store." Jake owned Elliott Paints, a store committed to serving and supporting the local economy, keeping houses bright and colorful, and entertaining pint-sized customers with paint swatches and wallpaper books. Trips to visit Jake at work had an intrigue I couldn't place but didn't fight.

"Daddy will be home soon, peanut." I capped my marker and rose from the table. "In fact, I'm sure he'll want to finish coloring this page with you."

"Noooooooo," whined Nora. "*You* have to finish it. It hasn't been fifteen minutes, Mom."

"But it *has* been five minutes," I said, hobbling to the kitchen with Nora clinging to my leg. Pink tulle billowed around her waist. "Nora, let go."

She slapped the floor with both hands. "No," she said, her eyes trained on mine and her bottom lip pushed out into a lump of sass.

I stopped. "Excuse me?"

"You're excused. Did you burp, Mommy?"

"Nora, did you just say no to your mom?" I crouched down to her eye level. Her lids were still smudged with purple shadow. The pouty mouth and kissable cheeks left over from infancy were tempting, but I did not allow myself to be wooed.

Nora looked toward the door, hoping either for escape or for Jake's entrance as distraction.

"Nora, when Mommy asks you to do something, you say, 'Yes, Mommy.'"

She said nothing, just stared at the door.

I turned her chin toward me. Her eyes remained fixed to the left.

"It seems to me you need a time-out to think." I scooped her up and headed toward The Time-Out Chair in the guest bedroom. Initially, we'd tried holding time-out in Nora's room. That stopped when I'd come in to see her standing on top of The Chair, naked and singing to a flock of toys, books, and dolls that had miraculously migrated to a neat row in front of her. The guest room had far fewer temptations, at least until she developed an interest in comforters and sheets with low thread counts.

"I'm sorry, Mommy," Nora wailed, thrashing her skirts into my face. "I'm ready to be nice! I'm ready to be nice!"

"I'm glad," I said, setting her down on the red chair. "We can talk about it when the timer goes off." I paused in the doorway. "I'll be back in five minutes."

"Six," she moaned through tears.

☾ ☽ ☾

Five minutes later the microwave timer beeped and I heard Nora call, "Am I done?"

Piling the chopped vegetables into a bowl, I turned on the burner and swirled oil into the wok. "Come into the kitchen, please." A better mother would have gone to her child and had a heart-to-heart about disobedience and how it breaks down the structure of a God-fearing society. But my wok was starting to smoke.

Nora stood in the doorway, not a tear in sight. Short-lived remorse, apparently.

"Nora, why were you in time-out?"

She twirled. "I don't know," she sang.

"Do you need five more minutes to think about it?" I asked as I stirred the meat sizzling in seasoned oil.

"I obeyed my mom."

"Disobeyed."

"Disobeyed."

"What do you say to me?" I turned from the stove.

"Sorry, Mommy," Nora said and ran to bury her face into my leg.

I crouched down to hug her. "I forgive you," I said into her curls.

"I forgive you, too," she said before prancing back to the table.

I shook my head and reached for the broccoli.

Close enough.

chapter/two

I met Jake Elliott on a college dare. His dare, not mine. It was a cloudy April afternoon and I sat alone at a cafeteria table piled with papers and books. Not a savory place, the cafeteria, neither for eating nor for meeting your soul mate. The walls were painted industrial pale green, high gloss so any errant flecks of gruel could be soaped and scrubbed without too much effort. The tables and chairs were made out of a very hard material known to survive nuclear blasts and the weight of the football team.

And the food . . *Food* was a term used loosely at the Caf. Label reading was key. Students would squint at greasy note cards taped onto plastic food shields.

"It says Moussaka."

"I think this one is a meat product."

"How about this: Scaly Surprise?"

For four years, I subsisted on PBJs and spaghetti. It was not a time of plenty.

That April afternoon I sat alone by the window, cramming for a three o'clock test in statistics. I abhorred stats, felt nauseous from my semester-long carbfest, and was waterlogged from rain that hadn't let up for a week.

In short, the conditions were ripe for romance.

"Excuse me," he said.

I looked up from my notes. I didn't recognize the speaker. He towered above my table, long and lanky, probably a baseball player, maybe a runner. Sandy blond hair, blue eyes, cut cheekbones. He wore the uniform of a college male in the late nineties: jeans, long-sleeved T-shirt, running shoes, and a worn baseball cap. A dark green windbreaker, still wet from the rain, cloaked his upper half. He shifted from one Nike to the other and didn't seem to know where to put his hands.

"Yes?" I asked.

He looked behind him. Several tables away, two guys sat watching and smirking. Windbreaker Guy turned back to me and lowered his voice. "Do you mind if I sit down?"

I gestured to the empty seat across from me. I glanced at my watch. Twenty minutes to test time. "Do I know you?" I asked.

"Not exactly. I'm Jake." He removed his cap and looked behind him again. The snickering boys were leaning forward in their chairs. Not ones for discretion, those two.

"Jake, I hate to be rude, but I have a test in twenty minutes and—"

"Right," Jake said. He laughed nervously. "You're probably wondering why I'm here."

I raised an eyebrow.

"I'll just cut to the chase." He ran his fingers through his hair. "See those guys over there?" He tossed a glance at the snickerers.

I nodded.

"I owe them some money and wondered if you could help me out."

Give me a break. "Sorry, bud. I can barely pay my own rent." I started packing up my things. Maybe I could finish studying as I walked to class. . . .

"I don't want your money," Jake said, offended. "I just need you to kiss me."

I looked up. "You're kidding."

"I'm afraid not." Jake sighed. "I owe them fifty each, and they agreed to forget about it if I could get you to kiss me. Here. Now." He bit his lower lip and watched my face.

I shook my head, tried to hide a smile. "Well. My kissing activity has never involved the exchange of funds. In fact, in some circles, this kind of activity could land you a night in the slammer. Selling one's wares and what have you."

Jake blushed. "Just one kiss. I promise. A quick one." He smiled shyly. "You'll barely even feel it."

My heart started pounding. I cocked my head and looked at his face for a moment. It was a nice face. I sighed. "All right."

He did a fist pump. The peanut gallery hooted and nearly fell off their chairs.

"Just one thing," I said, holding up my hand. "Don't I get a reward of some kind?"

"Absolutely," said Jake, nodding with enthusiasm. "Name your price."

I smiled. "I'll have to think about it."

"Fair enough," he said, then rose from his chair. "I think I'll stand. I mean, do you think we should stand? It's a little awkward across the table."

"I'm pretty sure the table isn't the problem," I said as I laid down my pen. I stood and took a step toward him.

"Whew," Jake said. "Okay. Here goes." He leaned toward me, closed his eyes, opened his eyes.

Good grief. He needed help.

I stood on my tiptoes and put one hand on his chest. He smiled and pulled me to him.

There.

I closed my eyes and felt his lips meet mine. They were full and soft. I smelled the remnants of an Altoid.

We pulled away and I opened my eyes. He was blushing. His friends were slapping each other on the back and cackling.

"Thanks," Jake said. His eyes were bright. A smile played mischievously on his lips. "You made that remarkably painless."

"You're too kind." I piled my books and papers into my backpack. "I'm glad to help you become debt free." Pulling on my coat, I said, "Nice to meet you, Jake."

"What about your compensation?" he asked as I started to go. "Can I take you to dinner?" Jake handed me my umbrella.

I smiled. "I don't know. Things are moving awfully fast between us."

He grinned. "I'm usually not this forward. I'm a math major."

I groaned, remembering my test. "Okay, Math Major With Poor Business Sense. I'll meet you at Sal's this Friday at seven." I walked away, giving high fives to the hecklers on my way out.

"Poor business sense?" Jake asked behind me. "What are you talking about? I just got a hot girl to kiss me *and* am free and clear of a hundred bucks I owed. I'm a freaking entrepreneur!"

I shook my head, smiling to myself.

"Wait!" Jake called when I reached the door. "What's your name?"

I looked back as I unsnapped my umbrella. "Heidi."

"You have nice lips, Heidi," he called.

Pushing the door open with my shoulder, I ducked into the rain and had to run to make it to class on time.

I aced that stats test and I met the man of my dreams.

All in all, not a bad day.

❧ ❧ ❧

"You say tomato, I say tomahto, you say potato, I say potahto. . . ."

I heard Jake's warble through the screen door. The aired-out, sweet breath of spring infused our house. Nora and I had welcomed every single one of the day's sixty-five degrees with giggles and relief that we'd made it. In the way only a Midwestern climate can, our stubborn winter had finally tired and left without even leaving a note. Springdale, the small city where we lived, was abruptly scrubbed and shiny, ready and willing for our first week of spring. I'd propped open the heavy front door of our hundred-year-old house and let the open screen usher in the first smells of green in months.

"Let's call the whole thing off," Jake finished as the screen door slammed behind him. I'm not one to talk, but even in my musically challenged head I knew my husband couldn't sing. It was awful, really. Nora, though, being the offspring of two croakers, thought singing was little more than slurring together the spoken word and that her parents were only a recording contract away from Andrea Bocelli and Charlotte Church.

"Daddy!" she squealed, dropping her markers and running to Jake.

"Hey, peanut," Jake said as he threw her into the air. "Did you miss me?"

"Yes, oh, yes," Shirley Temple replied, her halo placed just so. "I missed you *so much*, Daddy. You're the best daddy in the whole world!" Twirl for emphasis.

I cleared my throat. "Welcome home, superhero." I turned from the stove to kiss him, wooden spoon still in hand. "Must be nice to have your own slice of parent worship each time you darken our door."

"Jealous?" he asked, reaching for the pile of cashews waiting for their turn in my stir-fry.

"Yes." I slapped his hand away but not before he threw a handful of nuts into his open mouth. "*I* want a hero's welcome."

"Heroine's." Jake said, swiping a piece of beef out of the wok. "I love correcting a teacher's grammar." He wrapped his arms around my waist and looked over my shoulder as I cooked. "Maybe it's something about the naughty school-teacher fantasy, the wild woman caged behind nerdy glasses and a tweed suit."

"First of all, this is an issue of vocabulary, not grammar." I squirmed away to get three plates out of the cupboard. "And secondly, I don't own tweed."

Jake smiled and followed me to the table. "Whatever. I

know a heroine when I see one. And you're Nora's."

"That's sweet but a lie." I handed him napkins and silver-ware. "Nora," I called, "time to eat. Let's wash your hands."

Nora entered, preceded by the sound of swishing skirts. "Daddy will help me. Right, Daddy?" She clung to his legs as if the alternative was to be washed head to toe in boiling lye by the Wicked Witch.

"I'd love to help you, sweetie." Jake picked her up and headed to the bathroom.

I hummed the chorus to "Holding Out for a Hero" from *Footloose* as they left, though no one in our tone-deaf family could have told you that.

℮ ℈ ℮

I stared at the ceiling above our bed, trying to block out the sound of Jake's electric toothbrush. It beeped every thirty seconds to remind Jake to move on to the next quadrant. He loved it, just like he loved color-coordinating his closet, sharpening pencils, and getting his hair cut every four weeks to the day by a woman named Gladys.

Math major.

Nine nights out of ten, I was the first one ready for bed. There were two things at work here. First, conventional wisdom that women spend more time in front of the mirror was nothing but a myth. As much as they would like to deny it, straight men like primping just as much as gay men do. Gay men are just better at it. The second reason I was ready for bed before Jake was that at the stroke of nine o'clock, I could no longer speak in full sentences without my head drooping and puddles of saliva pooling on my collar. Some days I was even able to rewrite history in my head and forget the bone-weariness I'd felt teaching students how to say, *"Perdón, señora. ¿Dónde está el metro?"* But after spending my days enslaved to a toddler, the thought of having all those kids go home to their own parents at three thirty took my breath away.

"Sorry about the rice," I said from my pillow when Jake emerged from the bathroom. For all those minutes, you would have thought he'd smell like jasmine or be painted with henna or something. The only difference I could see was broccoli-free teeth and a red bump on his neck where he must have picked a zit. Don't let anyone tell you the marriage bed isn't a place of glamour.

"No problem," Jake said before dropping to the floor. I could hear him exhale as he began his nightly sit-up regimen.

I sighed, abs nice and squishy under the covers. "I can't believe I forgot to turn on the rice cooker. Actually, I can believe it, but I'm sorry you had to eat stir-fry with macaroni *sans* cheese."

Jake counted with each exhale. "No (*puff*) big (*puff*) deal (*puff*)."

It really wasn't a big deal. The marinated meat lost a bit of its appeal when cushioned by slimy macaroni, but Jake was game to eat nearly anything, and Nora wouldn't have eaten the rice anyway. Still, I felt the now-familiar frustration of getting only halfway done with everything I started. Martha made it look so easy, even during house arrest.

"Macaroni's cheap, anyway," Jake said as he crawled into bed. He turned off his bedside lamp and pulled me toward him. "How much was the beef?"

"I don't know . . . four, five dollars. Since when do you care about the going rate of sirloin?"

"Just wondering." He paused. "We should keep an eye on how much we're spending, that's all."

I tried to see his face in the darkness. "What does that mean? Is the store doing okay?" I thought of the certified letter I'd signed for. Jake had let out a quiet curse when he opened it, saying he'd forgotten to pay the electric bill. My husband had wholeheartedly supported my decision to take time off from teaching to stay at home with Nora, but it had also meant he became the sole breadwinner at the Elliott house. We'd had to cut out vacations and hadn't made any large purchases in a year and a half, but maybe things were tighter than I'd thought.

"We're fine," Jake said through a yawn. "Don't worry about it." He kissed me on my hair. "Love you."

That was my cue. "Love you, too."

Following his own advice, Jake's pretty little head was already deep into worry-free sleep before the count of twenty.

chapter/three

"Annnnnieeeeeee!" Nora threw herself with a flying leap into the arms of my best friend.

Annie pulled down her surgical mask and hugged Nora to her. "Hi, honey. How's my favorite three-year-old on the planet?"

"Almost four!" Nora said, already jumping out of Annie's embrace. "Aunt Annie, do you have treasures?" Nora looked around the lobby of Annie's office.

"Nora, manners, please," I said, shaking my head at Annie.

Nora straightened her back and gave Annie cocker spaniel eyes. "Please, Aunt Annie? Please do you have treasures, please?"

"I sure do," said Annie, taking Nora by the hand. "You may have as many treasures as you want, no matter what grouchy Mommy says." She squinted her eyes at me as they passed, daring me to defy a godmother the right to indulge.

"Give me a break," I muttered and followed the two of them through Annie's dental office.

Becca, Annie's receptionist, was taking a call at the front desk but smiled and waved at us as we passed. I heard her saying, "I understand, Mr. Connor, but I'm afraid it's not Dr.

Hepburn's fault that Koko chewed your lower denture. . . ."

The office was empty other than Becca and our threesome. Annie had called me at home that morning and asked that I come by during the noon hour. My closest friend since grade school, Annie ran a well-respected and bustling dental practice, one of the few female-owned in Springdale. The daughter of a farmer, Annie had worked hard to put herself through many years of schooling and build a successful business. Her office space reflected an attention to detail. The walls were painted a buttery yellow, no drips on the Berber carpet. White trim framed expansive windows I knew were cleaned, inside and out, each month. A series of watercolors hung in the hallway. Vibrant and fluid, the pieces had been painted by a local artist and depicted changing seasons on the prairie. I could almost see a freckled and braided Annie playing in the fields alongside her dad. Those paintings said much more about who she was than her purple scrubs and six-figure salary.

"Treasure found, my captain," Annie said as Nora ran and slid on her knees toward the "treasure box." To pacify kids who'd endured a trip to her chair, Annie offered a cardboard box full of plastic toys, whistles, and costume jewelry. Traditional patients were allowed to choose one treat; my daughter was given free reign. As if she needed any encouragement in her journey toward the throne.

"Let's bring this into Annie's office so Mommy and I can talk," Annie said, hefting the box into her arms. Annie was tall, blonde, and skinny as a result of hours of triathlon training. I'd already put in a request for her body in the afterlife.

"Thanks for stopping by," she said, closing the French doors behind her.

Elbow-deep in the treasure box, Nora had five strings of Mardi Gras beads around her neck and was rummaging for more.

"No hay problema," I said, taking the seat across from her desk. "What's up? And why are you acting like the room is bugged?"

She turned from her post at the door, where she'd been peering out the window. She walked to her desk and sat down on the edge of her chair. "I've made a decision," she said in a hushed voice.

"Can I guess?" I whispered.

Annie rolled her eyes. "I suppose. There's no way you'll get it."

"You're firing Becca."

"Of course not," she said indignantly. "Becca runs this place."

"Like a sergeant," I said. "Not that I don't like her."

"Every dentist knows a sergeant with a smile is the best possible person to man the front desk. Next guess."

"Okay, you've decided to ask out the hot anesthesiologist next door."

She pulled a face. "Absolutely not. He belongs to the NRA."

"So do most of the men in Pocahontas County."

"Exactly." Annie was likely the most sought-after bachelorette in Springdale. Many a male had tried and failed to capture her heart, even my own ex-boyfriend, Ben. He'd lasted the longest—nearly a year—but in the end, he simply couldn't keep up. Annie had too much spice and not enough neediness. "One more guess, Heidi," she said, voice still lowered and fidgeting in her chair. "I have a root canal in ten minutes."

Nora looked up from the box. Every one of her fingers held an adjustable ring, which was making it difficult to yo-yo. "Mommy," she whispered, "you have a good inside voice."

"Thank you, sweetheart."

She nodded and started lining up rubber lizards.

"Okay. My last guess," I said. I closed my eyes, lifted my chin. I heard Annie sigh impatiently. Opening my eyes, I said, "I know. You're going to ceramic tile your kitchen."

She shook her head, gave a small smile. "You see? You've only confirmed that I'm making the right decision."

"What decision? And how did I confirm it unknowingly?"

Annie took a deep breath. "I'm going to Europe. For a year."

I froze.

"Well," Annie said, eyes dancing. "What do you think?"

I shook my head. "I don't understand. You can't move to Europe."

"Yes, I can. And I will. In two weeks."

"*What?*" I felt my blood pressure rising.

"I know, I know," she said, crouching to open the mini-fridge by her desk. "It's pretty impulsive. But that's the point."

"But how? What about your practice?"

"I've already taken care of it," she said, opening a carton of yogurt and scooping up a bite. "There's a woman who graduated from dental school in December, a semester later than her classmates because she had a baby sometime along the way. She and her husband are thinking about settling in Springdale, so she's going to take over here while I'm gone to give the town a trial run. And there's a firm based in Milan where I can take temporary assignments to fill in for local dentists all over the continent. One, two weeks at a time, just enough to finance the trip. I'm telling the staff today." She smiled triumphantly.

"But a *year*?" I nearly squawked. "You can't leave for a year. What about *us*?" I looked at Nora, happily pulling the head off a lizard.

Annie put down her yogurt. "I know it sounds like a long time. But I have to do this while I have the chance." She pulled a chair up to mine. "Heidi, do you know what I bought in bulk last week?" She didn't wait for an answer. "Post-it notes. Do you know why? So I could make lists. I love lists. My whole life is a list of things I check off neatly at the end of each day. Maybe I should feel really great about how productive I am, but you know what?" She slammed her fist down on her desk.

Nora jumped.

"I don't feel productive at all," Annie said, getting up to pace. "I feel restless. Bored. And worst," she said, stopping to look me in the eye, "I feel old."

"Annie, for the love of Pete, you're thirty-three."

"My point exactly! At thirty-three, most women are married with three kids."

I raised my eyebrows at my one child.

"Or at least one." Annie hurried on. "For years I've waited for my life to come to me. But now it's time to go get it. No more Post-it notes. No more predictable, boring Annie. It's time for a change."

"Change is good," I agreed. "I love change. What's wrong with changing your kitchen tile?"

Annie smiled. "Hearing your guesses at the beginning of this conversation only confirmed how much I need to do this."

"Glad I could help," I said glumly.

"Your wildest idea of what I'd do was a weekend of home improvement. Don't you see, Heidi?" She sat down beside me again, took my hand in hers, and searched my face. "I don't want to get to the end of this and feel like I was *safe*. Can you understand?"

I sighed. I looked at my daughter, who wore pink John Lennon glasses, five strands of beads, the rings, and a feather boa. "Of course I do. Just because I'm blessed with a kid and husband doesn't mean my life is breathtaking on the excitement grid either." I met Annie's eyes. "I understand. Your world feels too small and you need to get out for a while."

"Exactly. Will you support me on this?"

"No, but I'll try really hard to fake it while I lick my wounds."

"Good enough," she said and kissed me on the cheek. "You can pout all you want after I board that plane in two weeks."

"I suppose you'll need help getting ready for this adventure thing." I made my voice sugary. "Anything I can do, don't you be afraid to give me a jingle, m'kay?"

"Heidi," Annie said, pleading with her eyes.

"All right, all right. I'll help you pack, shop for outlet converters, find foreign language dictionaries," I said. "Where in Europe are you headed, anyway?"

"I'm thinking Italy first, then Greece, Spain, maybe France."

"I hear Budapest is the new Prague," I said, helping Nora gather her booty.

"Really? Maybe I should consider Hungary." Annie swished some mouthwash and grabbed a fresh mask. "Thanks for coming in, Elliott girls."

Nora flung her arms around Annie's neck. "Thank you, Annie. I love my treasures."

"Come back anytime and get as many as you'd like," Annie said and kissed Nora on her forehead.

"That's right," I said, "as long as it isn't before you turn five. Aunt Annie will be busy eating baguettes and Brie until then."

Annie shot me a look.

Nora pranced out of the room, heavily adorned and clueless to the ways of best friendship.

"Sorry," I mumbled as I gave Annie a hug. "I'll have to work on censoring my nonsupportive comments."

"Love you," Annie said. She put her hands on my shoulders and looked into my face. "I'll miss you, Heids."

"Me, too," I said, my eyes filling. "You're leaving me all alone in NRA land."

She chuckled. "Yes, but it's still home."

"If I give you ruby slippers, will you use them when you're sick of gallivanting across the Old Country?"

"Of course," she said. We'd reached the front door. Becca was still on the phone, this time with a Mrs. Murphy, whose son had knocked out his front tooth in a bowling incident.

"Call me," I said as Nora and I walked through the door Annie held for us.

"I will," she said, smiling and waving at Nora before letting the door shut.

Nora grabbed my hand and we walked slowly to the car. I inhaled the scent of new grass and blooming daffodils, trying to picture a year without Annie.

chapter/four

Three years ago I met Jesus.

Now, before you get too nervous, I want to assure you I didn't actually *see* Him. That is, it wasn't like a bad mushroom trip or anything involving Pink Floyd. I just felt this stubborn tug toward figuring Him out, and He showed up, figuratively speaking. My heart knew, kind of like the sudden and forceful realization that I was living and loving on a whole new level the first time I saw Nora's face. I met Jesus and He hasn't ducked out on me yet.

My friend Willow says He never will. Actually, the Bible says that, but Willow has a knack for distilling the Bible into everyday language. She does tend to overuse phrases like "Right on" and "That *speaks* to me," but it's hard to shake the hippie inside. Willow became a Christian when she was an acid-tripping, free-loving commune dweller in the late seventies, so some of her most treasured images of Jesus still look tie-dyed and free-spirited.

"Do you know how to tie-dye?" I asked her the next afternoon over coffee at the art gallery/café she owns in downtown Springdale. The business was housed in what used to be an Episcopal church and exhibited the work of both national and local artists. I met Willow once a week for coffee in The Loft, a cozy lunch spot nestled in the former choir loft.

Willow looked up at me over a heavily caffeinated double espresso. Her mane of auburn curls spilled just over her shoulders. Warmth radiated from her freckled face, pink cheeks, and green eyes. "Do I know how to tie-dye? Are you kidding?"

I shrugged. "Don't all hippies know how to tie-dye?"

Willow laughed. "Speaking only for my own hippie self, I was not in any condition during my commune years to be trusted with garment dyeing." She sipped her drink. "Besides, I was more into muumuus, peasant shirts, and bell-bottoms."

"Righteous, man," I said.

She ignored me. "So how are things?"

This was my cue to start talking about how I was doing with the Jesus thing. "I'm doing okay. But I think God might be teaching me something hard. Not sure what yet, but it's not looking like an easy one."

Willow raised her eyebrows. That meant I should keep talking. All those years in touch with her feelings had made Willow a master of body language.

I cleared my throat. "Annie's moving to Europe. For a year."

"That's wonderful," Willow said, eyes sparkling. "What a great idea!"

I should have known Hemp Mama wouldn't be on my side. "Yes. It really is a great idea. For her."

Willow nodded slowly. "And you're miffed she's leaving you."

I avoided her gaze and took a swig of my peach mango tea.

"Well, this is excellent," Willow said, resolve in her voice.

"You're right. You're primed and ready for a life lesson. What are you going to do about it?"

I looked at her. "Get perspective from my spiritual mentor who doesn't tie-dye?"

She smiled. "Let's take a look."

After forty-five minutes, I was armed and ready to go. Willow had pointed me to a verse in the Bible where Jesus was telling His friends that He'd never leave them or forsake them. Of course, then He floated up into the sky and they stood staring at the clouds, but Willow said that was the point. That He was still with them, just not physically.

"So, what—Annie's with me even after she takes off in two weeks?"

"Afraid not," Willow said. "Jesus is the only one who can make that promise. But that means you're never alone. Ever."

I sighed. "What if I don't always feel like that?"

She smiled. "Faith has very little to do with feelings most of the time."

Willow would know. Her husband, Michael, died after a draining struggle with Lou Gehrig's disease. If she'd relied on feelings alone, she might have never uncurled from a fetal position, leaving her three boys to fend for themselves.

"But enough about me," I said as Willow drained the last drops of her espresso. "How are you?"

Willow sat quietly, looking past me. "It's been a rough week." Her eyes clouded. "The boys miss their dad in waves, but usually the waves hit at different times. This week they're in sync." She shook her head. "We'll be all right. I just thought the valley would be getting more sun by now." She smiled feebly.

"My problems are pathetic," I said, wincing. "Do you go home and think, 'Nice girl, but I wish she'd quit her whining'?"

Willow chuckled. "You're talking to the queen of whine. You aren't pathetic."

"Thou shalt not lie."

Willow's eyes widened. "Gutsy, darlin', quoting Scripture like that."

I grinned. "Learned it from my spiritual mentor."

"Fire her," she said, shaking her head. "The blind leading the blind."

I made her stand up and gave her a hug. "Do you see what you've accomplished?" I asked into her curls. "Three years ago I never would have voluntarily hugged a person in a public eating establishment." I pulled away and said, "You religious people are getting to me."

She smiled. "Quoting the Bible, hugging people. . . . Better watch out or you'll start giving all your worldly possessions to the poor."

I thought of our overdue electric bill and wondered if that left me off the hook. I shivered and said, "Don't talk like that."

She giggled. "See you next week."

☙ ❧ ☙

Most of the important things about motherhood were wisely kept under wraps from me until it was too late. Though sleeplessness was alluded to in vague terms ("Trouble sleeping in that last trimester just means your body's getting ready for baby"), no one told me I'd feel and look like roadkill for half a year. Pregnancy guidebooks warned I might feel "uncomfortable or nervous" about resuming sex, but they failed to mention that even if Jake could pretend he hadn't seen my body open like the Grand Canyon, I would feel about as sexual as a root vegetable. And that was on a good day—at least rutabagas respond to sunlight.

By far, though, the greatest failure in childbirth education was the idea that with diet and exercise a girl could reclaim her prepregnancy figure. Sarah Jessica did it. Madonna and Gwyneth did it. Even Rachel on *Friends* did it. It mattered not that Rachel was a fictional character and that Jennifer Aniston's "baby" was really a pillow peeking coyly above A Pea in the Pod drawstring pants, her stomach bronzed and free of stretch marks. What mattered was the volume of conclusive Hollywood evidence. Pregnancy was but an illusion, a brief interruption in one's quest to be bootylicious. In fact, having a child *enhanced* one's attractiveness, made one more of a woman, made one's sexuality bloom. Pregnant and blossoming, I told myself, I am beautiful! I am woman! I, too, will keep the boobs but lose the flab!

Turns out diet and exercise are not nearly as effective as a good airbrush.

And yet I soldiered on. Strut-n-Stroll was my weapon of choice. Each week I united with a throng of women intent on rewinding their physiological clock. We gathered Friday mornings for a two-mile jaunt accomplished while pushing strollers. Sandwiched within the walk were brief "toning breaks" where moms could do push-ups on park benches, calf raises on mall steps, and other such nonsense. I felt nothing short of ridiculous. At least today's weather had allowed an outdoor walk around the city park. Breaking a sweat seemed more natural in the open air than in front of Gap.

"And stretch, and stretch, and take it to the left, and *one*."

I took it to the left but used my right hand to toss Nora another book. She had plowed through roughly fifteen library books in the first ten minutes of our workout. The prognosis for her making it to mile two was not favorable.

"Can you feel it, ladies?"

I knew our Strut-n-Stroll coach, Laura Ingalls Wilder. This was not her real name, but she bore striking resemblance, even in Lycra capris and an oversized T-shirt, what with the tightly wound bun and lack of makeup. Laura and I went to the same church and were members of a Moms' Group that was on temporary hiatus. Our leader, Molly Langdon, had finally agreed to her husband's petitions to travel more and volunteer less in their retirement. She and Joe had headed out to I-35 in their RV to visit kids, grandkids, and friends along the way. Though no one had yet stepped up to take her place, it would not have surprised me if Laura Ingalls, eager beaver that she was, would campaign for the position.

"Okay, ladies, let's keep strollin'!"

We continued circling the pond in the middle of our downtown park. Two weeks of warmer weather had coaxed green grass out of hiding. The gentle slope leading down to the water was sprinkled with crocuses and daffodils. A few patches of tulips had escaped being devoured by rabbits and arched hopefully toward the sun.

"Missed seeing you Sunday, Heidi." Laura had sidled up beside me and was pumping her arms as she walked.

I inched over to avoid being struck. "Yes, Jake and I stayed home with Nora. She had a bit of a spring cold."

"Oh, that's too bad," Laura said, breathing in through the nose, out through the mouth. "Of course, my kids aren't allowed to stay home from church unless they have a fever above 102 or are vomiting."

Compassion dripped from her Lycra.

"Mommy," Nora said. "Are we going to the playground?"

"We sure will," I said, fumbling in the undercarriage of the stroller for the Etch A Sketch. "As soon as we're done with our walk."

"But I want to go *now*."

"I understand, Norie, and you're doing a great job being patient. We'll finish our walk and then go to the playground."

"No, let's go *now*."

"Nora," Laura interrupted in the voice of a drill sergeant. "You're very blessed to have such a nice mommy who takes you on walks. There are many children in the world who can't walk. Or who live in places where it's dangerous to walk. There are many children *without* mommies."

Good grief.

Laura gestured like Julie Andrews. "Isn't this a beautiful day to see God's creation?"

Nora looked at Laura blankly for a moment. Arms still pumping, Laura raised one eyebrow at my daughter.

Nora twisted further around in her stroller. "Mommy," she whined, "I want to go to the playground."

"I always say," Laura said loudly as we ascended a hill, "the child who's brought to church on Sunday shows it the other six days." She patted me on the back. "God rewards those who make church attendance a family priority. Even when it's inconvenient."

My cheeks were flushed and I could feel myself revving up to have words with our self-appointed religious conscience, but before I had a chance for rebuttal, Laura buzzed to the front of the pack to correct another walker on her heel-to-toe technique.

"You go to church with her?" A tall woman in a light turquoise baseball cap with brown trim had fallen in step beside me. Her cap had the letters SC monogrammed in brown thread on the front. She pushed a running stroller that held a baby girl.

I sighed. "I'm afraid so."

She lifted one hand from the running stroller and offered it as we walked. "I'm Kylie Zimmerman." Her lively brown eyes were lightly lined and shadowed, soft complements to full lips dusted with lip gloss.

"Heidi Elliott," I said, shaking her hand. I regained two-handed control of the stroller just before mowing through a hydrangea bush. Nora hooted through the brief off-road detour. "And this is Nora."

Nora squirmed around to face us. "A pleasure to meet you," she said and bowed her head slowly.

"The pleasure's all mine, Nora," Kylie said, trying to suppress a smile. She looked at me with raised eyebrows.

I rolled my eyes. "Princess obsession."

Kylie gestured toward her sleeping babe. The little one had tufts of chestnut hair. Long eyelashes and fat cheeks relaxed around pouting, slightly parted lips. "This is Brenna. She's eight months old." She shook her head. "I can hardly imagine her saying something like that. We're still working on 'Mommy.'"

"Calm before the storm," I said. "Unfortunately, verbal ability does not come with a built-in censor. Last week, for example . . ." I unwrapped a granola bar and handed it to Nora, ". . . we were walking in the mall and Nora sprinted ahead of me, trying to get me to chase her. I did not, so four stores ahead of me with her hands cupped around her little mouth, she yelled, 'I won, Mom . . . *and* you have diarrhea!'"

Kylie snickered.

"For the record," I said, "I had perfectly normal stools."

"Children do rob a girl of her pride, don't they?" Kylie said, still smiling.

"How many children do you have?"

"Just two. Brenna's older brother, Myles, is in second grade at Franklin." She adjusted her cap. "Two and done for us. We wanted a boy and a girl, and we got lucky. Plus, I'm plenty busy with the business." She turned to me. "What do you do, Heidi?"

Ah, The Question. Since deciding to stay home, the "What do you do for a living?" issue produced a conflicted reaction in me. I was proud of my choice to care for Nora. I was able to see her take her first steps and learn the alphabet. My arms were there to comfort her when she skinned her knees, and I was the one who taught her how to give Eskimo kisses. But the pay was horrible, entire regions of my brain lay defunct, and I often felt like going for a quick walk to Vegas.

So when asked The Question, I gauged the audience and picked from several responses:

a. "I stay at home with my daughter."
b. "I stay at home with my daughter, but I used to teach high school."
c. "I'm a teacher, but I'm on leave to stay home with my daughter."

Kylie seemed to have some sort of job outside the home, and yet the Strut-n-Stroll crowd was typically mom-friendly. So I took the middle of the road with letter *b* and said, "I stay at home now, but I used to teach high school."

She nodded. "I'm sure that's been an adjustment. I really appreciate how much a stay-at-home mom does. But I've found I *wither* without enough *me* time." She said these last words as if dangling a carrot in front of Seabiscuit.

My turn. "So what do you do?"

"Well, Heidi," she said, her eyes lighting up, "I help women achieve their dreams."

"That's, um, great," I said. I pictured Wayne and Garth singing "Dream Weaver" and had to bite my cheek.

"Yes, yes," she said, "it really is. I'm a very fortunate woman."

I felt her waiting for me to say something. I gave in. "And how is it that you help women achieve their dreams?"

She pointed to the letters on her baseball cap. "Solomon's Closet."

We'd stopped at the back of the group to join the other walkers in quad work.

Kylie took a deep lunge beside sleeping Brenna. Her legs were at least a foot longer than mine and tan, a lovely contrast to my own pasty whites. "Have you heard of us?" she asked.

I shook my head. Nora was staring at a double stroller holding sleeping twins. They were dressed identically and slept cheek to cheek.

Kylie began to recite. "Solomon's Closet is a life-enhancing, woman-affirming business opportunity that seeks to help people draw out their best selves." She flashed a sparkly smile. "It's changed my life."

Sirens were screaming stage-four warnings in my head, but like a moth to the flame, I asked, "How so?"

We'd begun walking again. The mother of the sleeping twins cast a glance back at me and Kylie, taking note of her cap. Maybe I imagined it, but I thought she sped up.

"Solomon's Closet has allowed me to have the best of both worlds," Kylie said, adjusting the sunshade on her stroller. "I'm able to stay home with my children but still use my creative energies to grow my own business." She turned her head toward mine and winked. "And, of course, the extra money doesn't hurt."

My eyes latched on to a ring on Kylie's right hand, a sapphire the size of a quarter, surrounded by diamonds. Perhaps the Closet was lined in jewels.

"Great workout, ladies," Laura said from the front of the pack. We'd reached the end of the two-mile loop and stood near a parking lot full of minivans. I glimpsed the playground through the trees that surrounded us. "See you next week. And remember: fiber, fiber, fiber!"

A barely audible groan rose from someone in the group, though everyone I saw was smiling. Maybe the groan had been mine.

"It's great to meet you, Heidi," Kylie said when we reached

her car. "I look forward to finishing our conversation—next Friday?" She hit the keyless entry button on her keychain. The doors of her silver Mercedes SUV unlocked.

"Um, sure," I said, turning toward the Beast, my 1987 Honda Civic.

I saw Kylie sneak a peek at my sweet ride before turning a last smile my way. "Or maybe we can have coffee sometime. I can tell you my story."

"Right," I said, trying to look casual, yet smashing, as I wiped sweat off my glistening forehead.

She waved and turned her attention to lifting Brenna into her car seat.

With Nora freed and the stroller folded into the Beast's trunk, I turned to my daughter. "To the playground. Thanks for being such a good girl during our walk, Norie."

She smiled and took my hand. "The pleasure was all mine."

chapter/five

There's a difference between owning a house and *living* in a house. Before I stayed home with Nora, my house was the place where I regrouped between work shifts. Since taking leave from teaching, however, I *knew* my house. I *dwelled* in my house. And I realized that pretty much everything needed to change.

Jake and I bought our two-story when we were young and stupid. The charm of living in a century-old home conquered any worries about rehab, overhaul, or upkeep. We fell head over heels for the oak staircase and floors, the wide picture windows, the leaded glass on the front door. The claw-foot tub in the bathroom screamed "bubble bath by candlelight." The butler's pantry planted seeds of culinary adventure. The large dining room promised leisurely meals surrounded by friends and family. And to top it all off, the price was right. As part of a city-driven move toward gentrification of older neighborhoods, we purchased the house for a song and with record-low interest rates.

Ah, but the fine print. Our euphoria chipped away gradually, starting with the first time I tried hanging a painting and ended up splintering off large chunks of wall plaster with a single nail. The tub was, in fact, a great bubble bath locale, but the only way to shower was by crouching in said tub and using a hand-held hose attachment, all the while trying to keep from drenching the walls with wild spraying. Jake found this particularly emasculating and found a plumbing shop that could special order a brass enclosure that hung from the ceiling and enabled a more dignified shower experience.

And about those special orders. We began the process of restoring our home with our sights set on architectural integrity, maintaining the character of the home even if that meant spending a few extra dollars to do it. Turns out "a few extra dollars" were rarely enough. The painter and his wife had stumbled into a project that could not be fixed with a coat of flat latex.

Even with the setbacks, however, Jake and I loved our crotchety old house and for the most part had enjoyed tackling one piece of the puzzle at a time.

Then came Nora.

Because our child-free moments were so few and far between, we were having to suck it up and live with lime green tile in the bathroom and pineapple wallpaper in the entryway. I was home now most hours of the day, thus increasing exponentially the amount of time I had to stew about tropical wallpaper. The minutes available for home improvement, however, had plummeted into our scary basement.

On this particular April afternoon, Nora and I sat in our most treasured spot: the front-porch swing. Crumbling walls aside, the people who had built our house a hundred years prior lived in a time when air conditioning hadn't eroded the social fabric of neighborhoods. Our porch was wide and welcoming, framed by a beadboard ceiling and a painted pine floor. My daughter and I had spent countless hours watching the world from the vantage point of our swing. On days when I cursed electrical wiring installed before Prohibition, I merely had to escape to our front porch for a reminder of why I loved our house. Nora had learned how to sit, crawl, and toddle around on our front porch. She'd scraped her knees there, fingerpainted there, and watched her first summer thunderstorm there.

And here we were again, another advent of a heartily welcomed spring. I wielded my broom like a weapon, sweeping a winter's worth of dust from the floor and brushing cobwebs from the ceiling. Nora sat on the steps with her dolly, Lois. Lois looked to be about five months old, never mind the elderly sound of her name. Lois had a twin brother, Jerry, but he was nowhere to be seen.

"Nora, where's Jerry?"

"Inside. He's in time-out."

That Jerry. Such a hellion. "What did he do?"

Nora was brushing Lois's creepy cornsilk hair. "He hit his mommy." She shook her head slowly. "Not in this house, young lady."

Ahem.

I gathered a small pile of brittle leaves into the dustpan. On my way down the steps toward the open bag of yard waste, I glanced at Nora and stopped. She'd pulled up her shirt and was suffocating Lois against her bare chest.

She looked up and caught me staring.

"What are you doing, honey?" I asked as innocently as a mother could when faced with her child's mininipple breastfeeding.

"I'm giving Lois my booby milk. She was crying."

"I see," I said, taking a seat by her on the step. "You're a very good mommy to Lois." I cleared my throat. "Did you see another mommy giving her baby booby milk?"

"Uh-huh. Olivia's mommy always gives her baby sister milk. She has biiiiiiiiiig boobies."

How lucky for her. I'd found lactation to lessen one's movie-star appeal in that department, but why burst any bubbles?

"Olivia's baby sister used to be in her mommy's tummy. I told her my mommy has a baby in her tummy, too."

Lori, Olivia's mom, lived a few houses down, and we took turns every so often providing child care so one of us could have an hour to herself. A wise woman, she'd suggested early on that I believe half of what was said about her and that she would return the favor. Still, I made a mental note to call Lori later and assure her there were only empty uteruses at the Elliott house.

"Mommy, when will my baby sister get here?" Lois was still eating her fill.

"Well, honey, probably not for a long time. I don't have a baby in my tummy right now. I'm busy taking care of my other baby."

"I'm a *big girl*, Mom," she said, as if *I* were the one who needed Velcro to keep my shoes on. "When my baby sister comes, you can give me Cheetos for a snack and I can give the baby milk from my boobies."

Interesting. "I'm sure you'll be a great helper."

Nora held up Lois to burp her. She gave a mock belch and set the doll down. "I'd better get Jerry out of time-out." She scrambled to her feet.

I tackled her when she tried to pass me. "Not before giving me a smooch." I blew raspberries on her neck while she tried to escape, arching her back in a fit of raucous giggling.

"Mommy," she said through laughter. "Jerry's crying."

"You'd better get him then." I planted one last kiss on her cheek and let her go. Watching her run inside to get the Jerrster, I realized that for the first time since bringing Nora home from the hospital, the idea of getting pregnant again hadn't made me wince or even do a preventative Kegel.

Maybe I was ready.

☙ ❧ ☙

I was reading in bed when Jake came swaggering in. I recognized that swagger.

"Whatcha doing?" he asked, starting to disrobe.

I looked over my reading glasses at him. "I'm reading. To relax before going to sleep."

His lips curled into a smile. "I know of much better ways to relax than a sorry book." Down to his boxers, he dove under the covers, ripped the book out of my hands and tossed it onto the floor. His hair was messed up, his face peppered with whiskers after thirteen hours away from a razor. He grinned. "You wanna?"

"Maybe," I said, taking off my glasses and reaching to put them on my bedside table. Jake followed me, moving the hair off the back of my neck so he could kiss it. I shivered and turned to him. "Don't you want me to change into something luscious?"

"Not really," he said, making a path of kisses on my collar-bone. "I'd just have to take it off."

I closed my eyes. Strut-n-Stroll was no Tae Bo, but it did keep me from feeling like a sloth. Sloths aren't very good in bed.

Jake spoke into my hair. "Hurry up and put in the goalie so we're ready to rock."

I lay motionless.

Jake lifted his face to look in my eyes. "Heidi?"

I tried to suppress my smile. "Maybe we don't need that pesky old goalie. Such a nuisance."

Jake's eyes got big. "Are you saying—you mean—you want to have another baby?"

I smiled, pulled him to me. "You always said to tell you when I was ready. I met another mom this week, and she had this beautiful little girl named Brenna. And then later Nora was breastfeeding Lois—"

"Who's Lois?"

"Lois, you know. Her doll? Jerry's twin?"

Jake shook his head. He looked overwhelmed.

I kissed his neck. "Listen, Nora's almost four, and I think I could do the whole baby chaos again. Maybe we should start trying." I watched his face for a response.

He pulled away. Running a hand through his hair he said, "Wow, Heids. I'm really surprised."

"Why aren't you smiling?" Why wasn't he smiling?

He lay back on his pillow, looked at me. "I am. I mean, I will. I mean . . ." He sighed. "I'd love to have another baby with you. I just wasn't thinking right now."

I turned onto my side, facing him, and hugged my pillow

to my head. "Well," I said slowly, "we'd have at least nine months to get used to the idea, right?"

"Right," he said, rolling onto his back.

We lay in silence for a moment, Jake looking at the ceiling and me looking at Jake.

"Jake, what's going on? Since when are you the one putting on the brakes? I'm the one with the womb, remember? No matter what the talk shows say, I'll be the one shouldering most of the burden here."

"That's not fair," Jake said, sitting up and throwing his legs off the side of the bed. "You should be careful tossing around statements like that."

I sat up and stared at his back. "Are you kidding? Do you really want to start tallying up how much each of us does in the realm of parenting to see who wins?" My skin was prickling with anger. "Jake, you wouldn't last *one day* doing what I do."

"Probably not," he said sarcastically, turning to face me. "And I'm sure we'd be raking in the cash if you were the sole breadwinner."

I stopped and stared, open-mouthed. "What does money have to do with it?"

Jake sighed, shoulders slumped. "It's been a rough month at the store."

My stomach turned. "April is usually one of your biggest months."

Jake nodded slowly. "Exactly."

"Jake, I had no idea. Why didn't you tell me things were tight?"

He stayed with his back to me. "I didn't want you to worry.

The winter was pretty slow, but winter usually is. March should have been better, and April should be comfortable. But our numbers are way below normal." He sat very still.

I came behind him, wrapped my arms around him. "Babies are expensive."

He nodded.

"So we wait."

He put his head down. I put my cheek on his.

"It will get better, honey," I said. "We'll be okay. I'll just fire the maid and stop buying so many furs."

He smiled. "We will need to cut corners."

"Absolutely," I said, hopping out of bed. I ducked into the bathroom for a moment and then came to stand in front of him. I pushed him onto his back. "I love cutting corners." I kissed his chest. "I'm actually a total cheapskate at heart." His neck. "In fact," his ears, "I'm especially fond of free entertainment."

A half smile curled one side of his mouth. "Is that right?"

I nodded. "Goalie's in position."

He kissed me gently, sweetly. "Thanks, Heidi."

"I love you," I said and wrapped myself around my financially strapped but undeniably handsome husband.

The seams in the road made a slow, rhythmic percussion in the car, the only noise as we traveled toward the airport in silence. Annie sat in the passenger seat, a small purse clutched on her lap. Briefly taking my eyes off the road, I glanced at her face.

"So this is it."

She nodded. "This is it." She gave me a crooked smile. "I

can't believe I'm doing this."

"Still time to back out." I raised my eyebrows hopefully at her.

She laughed. "Nora," she called to the backseat. "Will you tell your mommy to stop being so silly?"

"Don't be silly, Mommy," Nora said with cheeks packed full of grapes. We'd taken our snack on the run to get Annie to the airport on time.

"And tell her I'll write her on the computer."

"Annie writes a computer, Mommy."

"And tell her that I love you and Mommy very much."

"Annie loves Mommy, Mommy."

The road blurred and I wiped my wet cheeks. "Nora," I said, "will you tell Annie that we're very proud of her and that we'll miss her but that we support her decision and will wait with bated breath for her first correspondence and the many presents she'll bring back for us? I'd prefer Italian ceramics."

"Annie has presents!" Nora squealed, her smile allowing sloppy exit for a mashed-up grape.

Annie laughed and leaned over to kiss me on the cheek. "You and Jake, I tell you. Just a bunch of weepers."

"What did Jake say?" Annie had stopped by the store yesterday to say her good-bye to my husband.

"He got all teary and told me he'd mess up any smooth talkin' Eurotrash who bothered his surrogate little sister." She smiled, shook her head. "You got a good one, Heidi. A little sappy, but good."

I signaled to turn into Springdale Regional Airport. "You must be serious about this trip if even your best friends' weeping can't dissuade you."

We pulled to a stop under the departure sign. Four other cars were unloading passengers and luggage, but the sleepy airport was mostly empty. I pulled the latch to open the trunk and stepped out of the car.

Annie bounded out of the front seat and opened the door to Nora. She crawled in beside my daughter. I could hear her talking with Nora as I pulled Annie's huge suitcase out of the trunk and dropped it with a thud on the pavement. The bag had a front zipper, which I quickly opened to drop in a sealed envelope. I let the trunk slam shut, giving it an extra push with my fist to make sure it had caught.

Annie unfolded from the backseat and shut the door. I could hear Nora singing through the open window. Annie was brushing away tears. She came to stand in front of me and rested her hand on the handle of her suitcase.

"She's going to change so much while I'm gone," she said, retrieving a tissue from her carry-on.

I nodded. "I'm not very good at this good-bye drama." I shifted from one foot to the other. "Are you sure you're okay with us not coming in with you?"

She nodded, smiled. "Short and sweet is best. Just like an incision along the gum line."

"Sweet. I like thinking of bloody gums as a metaphor for our friendship."

She opened her arms and hugged me tight. I heard her take in a shaky breath. "Love you, Heids."

I swallowed hard and blinked like someone with a tic. "I love you, too. You're amazing."

She pulled away and hefted her bag up the curb. "You, of all people, know that's not true." Her grin was lopsided.

"I, more than anyone, know how true it is."

She took small steps toward the huge revolving door. "I'm going now. Missing the plane would be so anticlimactic."

"Call and write."

She waved to us. "Love you, Norie," she called. "Love you, Heidi."

"I love you!" answered Nora, waving wildly from the backseat.

I watched Annie walk away, waiting until she disappeared through the tinted glass.

℮ ℈ ℮

I stalked my e-mail until, twenty-six hours after our good-bye, Annie sent out an update.

From: anniebananie@wordlink.com
To: amorcita@springdale.net
Subject: All roads lead . . .

Heids-

I'm writing from the airport in Rome and all is well. Our plane flew in a slow circle around the city just as the sun was rising, and even though I'm dead-dog tired, I can't wait to get started exploring.

Thanks for the ride to the airport. I'll write more soon.

A

PS: You can stop watching CNN for news of international plane crashes now. Love to you, my neurotic best friend, and kisses to Norie.

chapter/six

It took a week to get my A-game back after taking Annie to the airport. I'd underestimated how emotionally draining it could be to ship one's best friend off to another continent. The next Friday morning, Nora and I slumped in defeat at the breakfast table. She mirrored my electrified hair and bleary eyes. We sat in silence, crunching on Grape-Nuts and looking up only when Jake set down his bowl with a clatter and poured milk onto his Wheaties. He flipped open his Bible and propped it around his bowl. Moving a mouthful of cereal to his cheeks, he said, "There's some wacky stuff in here."

In a moment of New Years hysteria, Jake had decided to read the entire Bible in a year. We'd been in the bookstore sometime in late December and he'd arrived at the cashier gripping a Bible edited for that purpose. Then and now I thought him nuts. It was enough for me to wade through passages involving actual people and story lines, but he'd been at it for months and had told me mostly about grain offerings and ranting prophets.

After several moments of silent reading, Jake took a swig of orange juice and said, "What do you think about concubines?"

"You thinking about getting one?"

Jake shook his head. "One woman in this house is plenty." He smiled at Nora. "I mean two. Sorry, peanut."

Nora looked at him blankly and kept sucking down her cup of juice. Like her mother, Nora is not a morning person.

Jake slapped the Bible shut and rose from the table. I watched him rinse his bowl in the kitchen sink. He wore a pair of flat-front khakis and a light blue checked button-down. I wasn't close enough to confirm it, but I knew he smelled of soap and toothpaste, ready for a day in the real world.

"Must be nice to go to work and get paid." I pushed my Grape-Nuts into a soggy lump in the center of my bowl.

Jake rejoined us at the table and gave Nora a kiss on the top of her head. "What are my girls up to today?" He kissed me on my cheek. The man knew the relational minefield I'd planted for him with my last comment.

I pouted in my pajamas. "Oh, you know," I said and sighed. "The usual. Thirteen-hour shift, infrequent adult interaction, no feedback on the exceptional job I'm doing, advanced bottom wiping and time-out granting."

Nora's eyes got huge. "I have a time-out?"

"No, honey. I was talking to Daddy."

"Daddy has a time-out?" Now she looked like she needed her thyroid checked.

"Yes," Jake said, tickling her under her armpits. "Mommy wants Daddy to go to time-out because he has a job to pay for your orange juice."

"Not true. I want you in time-out so *I* can take a turn being a grown-up."

"Wait," Jake said more loudly to be heard over Nora's giggling, "aren't you meeting Willow for lunch today?"

"Maybe," I mumbled. Sometimes a girl just has to hold on to a foul mood past the point of reason.

"All right," Jake said. He plopped Nora back into her chair and went to get his jacket. "I know when the battle is lost. I'll see you two tonight." He pulled open the front door and cool, damp air seeped into the house.

"Have a good day, honey," I sang. "You bring home the bacon and I'll just keep frying it up."

Jake shut the door with a dull thud and locked it behind him.

My point exactly.

℮ ℈ ℮

"And two glasses of the house white," Willow said before shutting her menu. "On me," she added when our server left.

"Thanks, but what's the occasion?" I unfolded my napkin and lay it across my lap. Willow had suggested lunch out this week instead of coffee at The Loft. Good to check out the competition, she'd said.

"We're celebrating," she said with a shrug. "What? Do you need me to give you a reason? Okay." She looked upward in thought. "Let's see. We're celebrating your first full week of survival without your best friend on the same continent."

I nodded. "I've only wept twice and succumbed to emotional eating three times. I feel I'm growing."

Willow took a sip of ice water. "Number two: Isn't Nora's fourth birthday coming up this month?"

"Yes, it is," I said, "and what better way to celebrate a child's birthday than to have lunch without her?" God bless babysitters the world over.

Willow smiled. "And one more thing: I'm celebrating Michael's and my nineteenth wedding anniversary."

My face fell. "Oh, Willow."

She shook her head. "No, actually, I'm doing really well this year. The boys have been particularly sweet. They made me breakfast in bed this morning." She smiled. "Charred toast, microwaved bacon, and root beer. We were out of juice."

"They're good kids."

"They got that from their father." Willow fingered her wedding band. She glanced around the restaurant and lowered her voice. "What do you think of this place?"

I took stock of our surroundings. Willow had chosen a new joint on the west side of town. Zucca's was a noodle bar, offering a full menu of variations on the pasta theme. They also served salads, soups, and desserts, all in completely inappropriate portion sizes. Zucca's hadn't been notified of America's problem with obesity.

"Too cold for my taste," I said. This was a slight exaggeration, what with my loyalty to The Loft. But Zucca's color palette was a bit too Japanimation for me: bright primary colors, silver painted chairs and tables, orange and red plaid linoleum. Light fixtures and serving counters shone with brushed platinum. The servers wore bright blue long-sleeved T-shirts with "Wanna caNOODLE?" in small white lettering on the back.

Willow nodded slowly. "We'll see how they do with an Alfredo. I'm guessing it will be as thick as Elmer's Glue."

I shuddered. "Have you ever considered opening The Loft for dinner?"

"Why, no, Heidi, I *haven't* seen that new Jessica Lange film," she said loudly, arching her eyebrows toward our waiter, who'd approached the table with two glasses of wine. She smiled sweetly at him. "Thank you, Aaron, is it?"

"Yes," said Aaron, nodding toward his name tag. He smiled. "Your meal should be out in a few minutes." He headed to the next table to clear empty plates.

"Jessica Lange?" I asked when Aaron was out of earshot. "What movie was that exactly? *Tootsie* with Dustin Hoffman, circa 1982?"

"Hush," Willow said. "I had to think fast. I didn't want to blow my cover."

I was about to ask her if she preferred *O Pioneers!* or *Cape Fear* when we were interrupted.

"Willow and Heidi!"

Willow stopped midsip of her Chardonnay to see Laura Ingalls scooting toward our table. Her hair was in a tight French braid. She was in navy blue from blouse to clogs but had really jazzed things up by slapping on clear lip gloss. A plain blonde woman followed closely behind.

"Hello there," Willow said, smiling at the two women.

"Heidi, Willow, meet Marilyn Lawrence, a dear friend and sister in Christ."

Marilyn extended her hand. Her mouth was drawn into a straight line. "Praise Him," she said, nodding to each of us as she shook our hands. She wore a tan corduroy jumper and Keds of the same color.

"Out for a ladies' lunch?" Laura asked and stopped abruptly. She cleared her throat. "I'd forgotten you were a drinker, Willow. And in the middle of the day, no less." She cocked her head to one side, looking an awful lot like someone picking a fight.

Willow laughed softly. "A drinker? I'm not sure about that, but I do enjoy a good glass of wine." She gestured to the table next to ours. "Would you two like to join us? There's plenty of room."

Marilyn shifted from one Ked to another, scanning the exits.

"Oh, no," Laura said. "We'll get out of your way." She linked her arm through Marilyn's. "See you at church this Sunday," she said, pulling Marilyn with her to a table across the room.

Willow chuckled. "A drinker. What a riot."

I looked at my glass of wine. "What was that all about? That Marilyn character looked like you'd asked her for an organ donation."

Willow rolled her eyes. "People are very funny, Heidi. And sometimes Christians are the most trying on my patience." She nodded toward Laura and Marilyn, who had joined hands across the table and were bowed deeply in prayer. "She single-handedly got First Lutheran to switch the Communion wine to grape juice. Said she was worried about alcohol consumption in the house of God."

"What do you think about that?"

Willow sighed. "I think I'd hate to see her under the influence, so it's probably a good thing." She smiled. "Once I tried asking her about Jesus' choice to turn water into wine instead of the other way around, but she started quoting rapid-fire Proverbs involving debauchery, so I let it go." Willow leaned over the table and looked me in the eye. "My advice to you is to seek God for yourself. All your life you'll hear people trying to steer you one way or the other, many of them claiming to have the market on truth. Take everyone—your pastor, your church friends, your flaky spiritual mentor—with a gracious grain of salt and then ask God yourself."

I nodded and took a sip of wine, but not before I turned in my seat to block Laura's view of my imbibing. "You are pretty flaky," I agreed.

Willow smiled. "And you're a quick study."

Aaron appeared and set down our dishes with a flourish. "One chicken fettuccini Alfredo and one rigatoni with tomatoes and capers. Would you ladies like another glass of wine?"

Willow caught my eye and snorted. "No, Aaron, I think we've been cut off for the day."

e ə e

There comes a time for every parent when the singular goal of the day becomes avoiding a call from Children's Services. If I can only make it until bedtime, I said to myself that afternoon. If I can just not kill anyone or harm myself, I will be victorious.

I'd thought my spiritual awakening would have taken care of these things. Wasn't Jesus supposed to make me nice? Wasn't He always talking about us being sheep? I knew sheep were rather stupid, and I could accept that, but weren't they also docile? Soft and snuggly? On this particular afternoon, I identified much more closely with Eden's serpent.

"Nora Hope Elliott, put down that marker this instant.

We do not write on the walls, and you know it."

"But Mommy—"

"'But Mommy' nothing. Put it down."

"I was just — "

"*Nora!*" I roared.

She stopped, marker in fist, and stared. Her blue eyes widened and her mouth hung open.

I stared back, clenched my jaw. "Put. It. Down."

She lowered her arm as if she were about to be frisked.

"Mommy," she said, shaking her head of curls. "Would you like to try that again in a nice voice?"

That's the thing with children: You teach them right from wrong and they turn around and use it against you.

I sighed and lowered myself to sit beside her on the hardwood. "I'm sorry, Norie. I'm not feeling so great today."

She pushed off the floor to a standing position. "I know, Mommy! I'll be right back." She scurried into the kitchen, and I could hear her rummaging in the pantry. A moment later, she reappeared with an empty white plastic bag from Tom's Ideal Grocery.

"Here," she said, pushing the bag into my hands. Then, in a singsong voice that I assumed was to mimic mine, she said, "Now, it's not fun to throw up, but it will help you feel better."

Nora had suffered through the stomach flu earlier that winter and we'd never stopped reliving the trauma of vomit. "Thank you, honey," I said, "but that's not the kind of sick I feel."

She scrunched up her face. "What kind of sick is it? Do you have a feeber?"

I shook my head.

"Headdick?"

"No," I said. "I think I just feel sad today. Do you ever feel sad?"

She crawled up on my lap and made a great show of making herself comfortable. "Oh, yes. I feel really, really, *really* sad when I'm in time-out." She shook her head mournfully. "And when Ursula the Sea-witch steals my voice." At this, she began singing the ascending scales of Ariel at full volume.

"Nora," I said above the drama, "I have an idea. How about we take out The Box?"

"Yippee!" Nora said, jumping up and running to her bedroom. I followed and reached up to the top shelf of her closet, pulling down a large box covered in pink and green polka dots and tied with a wide ribbon. The Box was the lazy mom's version of scrapbooking. I considered it a giant leap that I'd bought the ribbon and, in a surge of maternal motivation, had decorated the box with dots. The surge had ended as abruptly as it had begun, and under the lid was a jumbled pile of photos of the previous three years.

"Find the big belly ones," Nora instructed, bouncing up and down beside me.

I rummaged for a moment and came up with a full body shot of me, eight months pregnant and baring my swollen belly for the camera. If I'd looked, I would have found eight other photos of me in the same position, standing with my side to the camera and holding up fingers to correspond with my months of pregnancy. In the first four or five of these shots, I looked happy and expectant, pleased with my fattening frame. By month seven, however, my smile was forced and my expression bordered on hacked. I chuckled as I studied the photo from eight months, remembering how Jake's chipper attitude had made me want to mangle the camera. A month later, he'd had to bribe me with an hour-long massage to get me to cooperate with the final photo in the series.

"Was I in Mommy's tummy?" Nora asked, her nose inches from the image.

"Yes, you were," I said. "You kicked and kicked all the time. You loved swimming around in there, especially at night."

She nodded, familiar with the story. "Let's find the spaghetti one."

In one corner of the box, I saw a flash of red sauce and fished out a photo of Nora at ten months, arms up and a huge grin on her face. She sat in her high chair and had covered nearly every centimeter of her surroundings with spaghetti and marinara, face and hair included. In the time since that photo was taken, Nora had become something of a priss, so for her, this photo was like watching a Quentin Tarantino movie. Hated to look but couldn't pull herself away.

I riffled through the stack. Nora and her first trip to the park, Nora leaning like the Tower of Pisa as she learned how to sit. One of my favorites was a close-up of Jake and Nora, cheek to cheek and grinning at the camera. Nora was about five months old and already looked more like Jake than me, her curls starting to lighten and blue eyes shining like his.

I was surprised to feel a lump in my throat.

"When did you get to be such a big girl?" I asked, pulling Nora to me.

She squirmed away and said, "Mommy, do you have a baby in your tummy yet?" She reached over and pulled up my shirt to check for herself.

"No, peanut. No baby right now." I took a deep breath and let it out slowly. "Maybe someday."

"I need a baby sister so I can feed her with my boobies."

I was going to have to talk with Lori. This peer pressure to lactate was getting to be a bit much.

"Norie," I said, suddenly excited, "can you help me with something?"

"Sure, Mom," she said, watching me toss the photos back into The Box and lift it as I rose to my feet.

I offered my free hand to my daughter. "Bring your markers," I said and steered her toward the kitchen table, armed with a pile of memories, an artistic almost-four-year-old, and a plan.

chapter/seven

You know the adage about the way to a man's heart? I'd always thought that prescription was too primitive, even insulting. At the very least, the road map should acknowledge a detour to the bedroom. But the farther along in married life that I got, the more I knew Jake to be a man of simple pleasures. In the beginning, we'd relish entire evenings meticulously sorting out the crevices of our minds, the fascinating ways in which we were alike and different, our favorite characters from *The Goonies*, and whether we preferred Twinkies or HoHos. We'd look deep into each other's wrinkle-free eyes and profess our undying love and our astonishment that God had been so good as to make the other.

Somewhere along the line, and I couldn't pinpoint exactly when, we skipped the undying love part and went straight for a good burger. I can hear all the young lovers, wherever they are, gasping in disapproval and vowing never to stoop to the time when a satisfying meal ranks right up there with "I love you, Sweet Babycakes Darlin' Buttercup Munchkin Lovah." But the view was just as grand on the other side. In fact, sharing a meal with the man I love had become one of life's sweetest rewards for making it this far in the minefield of marriage. Turns out all that crevice sorting only went so far until we got hungry.

So with that in mind and with a few years of cooking under my belt, I set about preparing my case via the kitchen. The house swelled with persuasion: pistachio-stuffed chicken with apricot-mango chutney, spinach salad with toasted pecans and strawberries, garlic mashed potatoes, and home-made Texas dinner rolls. The grand finale, chocolate lava cakes to be served with vanilla bean ice cream, was quivering in sugar-dusted ramekins in our fridge. I finished slicing strawberries for the salad and inhaled the apricot-infused warm air permeating the kitchen. It had taken me four times as long as it should have to get this meal together, what with the gum-in-the-hair incident, the I'm-too-mature-for-naps scene, and the using-Scotch-tape-as-a-weapon episode. But the end product was turning out as I'd hoped. I breathed a prayer that my basting, dicing, browning, and whisking would not be in vain.

I peeked my head into the family room to check on Nora. She sat on the couch, accompanied by two rows of stuffed animals dutifully watching *Sesame Street*. Public television and the dinner hour was one of my favorite pairings. I snuck by before Nora could see me and remember she was hungry.

The front door opened to an early spring evening. Soft light spilled into the entryway and onto my husband. He gave a weary smile as he hung his jacket on the coatrack. "Hi, hon." He leaned down to kiss me. "What's cooking in here, hot stuff? Good grief, it smells amazing."

I smiled and returned to the kitchen. "Nora's in the family room," I said. "Five minutes to dinner, okay?"

I set the table with a vase of lilacs and even lit a candle.

Nora came running into the dining room and careened to a stop with her arms around my legs. "Mom," she whispered loudly. "Can I show him?"

"Not yet," I whispered back.

"What's with all the secrets around here?" Jake walked to Nora and lifted her upside down. She squealed fake protests. "You girls keeping secrets from me?"

"Yes," screamed Nora, giggling uncontrollably.

"Time to wash hands," I said. "We can talk about secrets after we've started eating."

Nora made it halfway through grace before blurting, "Surprise, Daddy!" Not waiting for a response, she scrambled back down her chair and ran to her room.

Jake's face was a question mark. I deferred with a small smile and a shrug. When Nora returned, her gait was regal and slow. She held a sheaf of papers bound loosely with ribbon and covered front and back with markered drawings.

"Your Majesty," she said to Jake.

He took the book, stopping to let Nora kiss his wedding ring. Who knows where she picked that up. Poor kid — all she wanted was a monarch in a land of plain old democracy.

"Thank you," Jake said, holding the book to the side of his plate and scanning the title. "'Fat Cheeks and Drool Stains: A Nora Elliott History.'"

"That's me," Nora said, crawling up on Jake's lap. They leafed through the sheets together, sharing Jake's dinner as they read. Nora provided page-by-page analysis, pointing out her favorites among the photos we'd included. Jake took turns responding to Nora's color commentary and silently reading the script I'd written at the bottom for his eyes only. I tried gauging his reaction but he gave nothing away. It was enough to keep up with little Joan Rivers.

"In this picture, I'm eating peaches and pears and I have *three teeth*. Can you believe it, Daddy? I have more teeth now and I can eat macaroni and bread and — "

"And my chicken?" Jake asked, watching her help herself.

"Nora," I said, reaching over to pull her off Jake's lap, "let's let Daddy finish the book by himself while you eat *your* dinner."

"But, Mom, I have to *'splain* it."

"If I have any questions, I'll sure let you know," Jake said, spearing a bite of salad. "Heidi, this tastes great," he said with his mouth full. He shook his head and let one side of his mouth upturn in a smile. "You're good, Elliott."

I smiled into my roll. "I'm glad you see it that way."

He got up to refill his glass of water. En route, he leaned down to kiss me. "We'll talk after she's in bed," he said softly into my ear. He moved to Nora and planted a loud kiss on her cheek. "Miss Nora, you're quite the artist."

"Thank you, Your Majesty," she said, and when his back turned she said to me, "I thought the king was supposed to say, 'Off with your head.'"

"Only when you don't eat your spinach," I said and began an impatient wait for bedtime.

℮ ℈ ℮

"Pretty sneaky, huh?" I asked when Jake and I curled up on the couch with plates of cake and steaming mugs of decaf. "You had a poker face as you read what I wrote."

He shook his head. "It's a darn good thing, too. Can you imagine the help we'd get from Chatty Cathy when she found out we were discussing family planning?"

"She's really into babies. What with baby Jesus, the baby who's almost stolen in *Rumpelstiltskin*, and Lori's breastfeeding, she thinks she's pretty much got the whole thing nailed."

He took a careful sip from his mug. He swallowed slowly, leaned forward to place his cup on a coaster, and looked at me. "Shall we go over the Top Ten?"

I nodded. "Hit me."

He opened the book to the last page and read aloud. "The Top Ten Reasons Heidi and Jake Elliott Should Set About Conceiving a Child." Jake looked up at me. "A nice touch, I must say."

I smiled. "Number Ten."

"'Number Ten,'" he read. "'Heidi's good in bed.'"

"An undeniable fact, but admittedly low on the priority scale."

Jake snorted. "I think you should be docked points if you're extolling your own bedroom prowess."

"Now just wait. Number Nine should clear me of all wrongdoing."

"'Number Nine,'" he read. "'Jake's even better in bed.' Okay, you're off the hook."

"Thank you."

"'Number Eight. We are young and energetic, which, while closely related to Numbers Nine and Ten, also means we should have more children before we're too tired.'"

"Exactly."

"Energetic but poor?" Jake asked.

"Patience, please."

"'Number Seven. Interest rates are at all-time historic

lows.' What, so we take out a loan? We roll our retirement funds into a Roth IRA?"

I shrugged. "It was the best I could do in financial-speak. There's more."

Jake sighed. "'Number Six. Nora is ready to breastfeed.'"

"And she's potty trained, so we'd only have one in diapers."

"Diapers are expensive."

"Well, we could always do cloth, and you could be in charge of the poopy ones."

"Moving on. 'Number Five. Heidi will do a much better job of clipping coupons and being generally frugal. She promises to swear off Raspberry Smoothies and Double Celestial Mocha Blasts, for example. And she'll quit smoking.'"

I smiled. "I'm ready to sacrifice."

"You don't smoke."

"But that would be really expensive, see? I just wanted to point out how much we *could* be spending and how much better off we are because we're not."

Jake sighed. "'Number Four. We love being parents and we're pretty good at it.'" He looked up at me with a slow grin. "No argument there."

"It gets better. Number Three."

"'Number Three. As the enclosed photos demonstrate, we have a very cute child and would be performing a service to society to procreate again. Plus, don't these images remind you of how much fun it is to have a baby in the house?'"

Jake flipped through the pages for another look. He stopped at the picture of Nora and him cheek to cheek. He shook his head and smiled. "She is so freaking cute."

I bit my lower lip to keep from smiling. Couldn't celebrate victory prematurely.

"'Number Two. Heidi will get a job.' What are you talking about?"

"Well," I said, "I've been thinking, and I have a few options. I could work at the bookstore part-time."

"Who would take care of Nora?"

"Rina?"

Jake looked at me in disbelief. "The German automaton?" Rina had cared for Nora when I'd gone back to teaching after my maternity leave. Her greatest strength was her immovable disposition. This was also what made her a little disturbing.

"What about Willow? I'm sure she'd help us out."

Jake shook his head. "I don't know if you want to mix business with friendship. Plus, she has a gallery and café to run."

I sat quietly for a moment, noting for the millionth time how nice it would be to live closer to family. Though, I reminded myself, proximity to my family and all its charming dysfunction would probably create more problems than it would solve.

"There's another option," I said. "I met this woman at Strut-n-Stroll. Her name is Kylie, and she's involved in some business called Solomon's Closet. Direct sales. Multilevel marketing, whatever."

Jake's eyes got big. "What, like a pyramid scheme? Heidi, you can't be serious."

"Just hold on," I said. "She seems pretty normal, law-abiding. And she drives a nice car, always looks put together. She says it's changed her life and that she's making money while staying home with her kids."

Jake looked like I'd just told him Elvis would be coming to stay for the weekend. "I can't believe I'm hearing these words coming from my wife's mouth. My wife, who got physically ill when forced to sell magazine subscriptions for junior high band."

"I know, I know. I usually hate selling things," I said. "But the stakes are different now. I'd be able to keep staying home. And have another baby. Plus, maybe I've just never sold the right product. Maybe if I really like what I'm selling I'll be better at it."

Jake took a deep breath. "All right. We'll think about it."

My heart soared. The job thing was going to be the hardest sell, so I was teetering on the brink of a successful pitch. "Number One."

Jake returned to the book. "'Number One. Heidi's been praying about it and thinks God's on board.'" Jake looked up. "Really?"

I nodded and sat up straighter. "Really. I mean, there was no parting of the Red Sea or anything, but I haven't gotten any red lights."

Jake nodded. "I've been praying, too, and have only gotten greens."

"Are you serious?" I said too loudly. My screech echoed off the wood floor. I lowered my voice and said, "You mean you were still considering this? Even after the goalie talk and the concerns about money?"

He smiled a crooked smile and ran a hand through his hair. "I was still kicking and screaming a bit, not understanding how God was going to work out the numbers. But you're right.

And I think we need to act on God's nudging and believe Him to be faithful like He's always been." He shuddered slightly. "This is not the way a math major likes to do business."

I jumped onto his lap and smothered him with kisses. "Thank you, thank you." I burrowed my face into his neck. "I'm more excited than a Pointer Sister. And I just can't hide it." I pulled my face away and looked into his eyes. "Ah, the powers of female persuasion."

"Yeah, right," Jake said, rising from the couch with me in his arms. He carried me down the hallway. "Don't start taking credit for God's work, you blasphemous woman."

"Absolutely not," I assured him. "But His mysterious ways can include chocolate lava cakes and a book of photos."

"Fair enough," he said, lowering me onto the bed. "Shall we, then?" he asked, his eyes shining.

"We shall," I said and pulled his face to mine.

chapter/eight

Late that night, I was unable to sleep through Jake's snoring. Our bed rumbled with his heavy slumber. Jake wasn't a chronic snorer, but when he did, I could feel my teeth vibrate. I tried kicking him, rolling him over. I even considered hunting down a twenty-four-hour pharmacy for one of those nose patches. After a good ten minutes of dramatic sighs heard by no one but myself, I threw off the covers and padded down to the computer desk in the basement. Most of the lower floor was downright spooky: stone foundation built with a mishmash of sizes and colors, the mortar crumbling to the touch; cracked cement floor; cobwebs that hung in lazy arcs in the dark wood beams overhead, no matter my weekly sweep of the place. The only space habitable by humans was a tiny room built into one corner that we assumed had once been used as an extra pantry. We'd violated fire code and hooked up two halogen lamps that brightened the gloom with the flip of a switch. The pantry shelves were stocked with books, and a fuzzy rug gave warmth to the room and to our feet. Add a chair, a desk, and a couple of picture frames, and we'd resurrected a small bit of good from a pit of scary.

Pulling a blanket around me, I settled into the desk chair and wrote a late-night e-mail to Annie. The next morning I received a reply:

From: anniebananie@wordlink.com
To: amorcita@springdale.net
Subject: Ready to rock, Italian style

Heidi —

Listen, I've had those lava things myself, so I can imagine Jake was a pushover. I'm excited for you two. I'm ready to spoil another Elliott offspring.

Rome is phenomenal. Sorry it's taken awhile for me to write again. I needed a few days to get my bearings, but I've found an Internet café close to my hotel, so I'll be checking my e-mail, at least while in Roma.

It's a strange thing to be here. I'm feeling equal parts exhaustion and exhilaration. Jet lag is still dragging me through its mud but I'm trying to convince my body to acclimate to a new time zone. Even went for a run this morning, though it felt more like training camp for the Marines. When I wasn't dodging Fiats that appear to adhere to some unwritten, hysterical "safety" code, I was preoccupied with not twisting an ankle on cobblestone streets. Might not try that again until I know the lay of the land.

It's been two weeks since I've worn latex gloves and I could not be happier!

Tomorrow morning I'm off to Vatican City and St. Peter's Basilica. I'll say a prayer about Baby Number Two (but only if it doesn't get in the way of meeting Giuseppe, my Italian prince. My piety is fickle when it comes to royalty).

Still love you and miss you already.

Ciao!

Annie

PS: Thanks for the ruby slippers postcard. I keep it by my bed and know the magic words for when the time comes.

That afternoon Nora helped me write back:

From: amorcita@springdale.net
To: anniebananie@wordlink.com
Subject: Love from Jerry and Lois

Dear Aunt Annie,

This is Nora. My mommy is touching the letters and I'm talking. How is your trip? We love you. Today Jerry and Lois are coming to the park with me. Did you ride in an airplane? Remember the time you swinged me really fast in a circle and I threw up?

Bye, Annie!

Nora

PS: The Mother also sends greetings and her love, though she will keep her throw-up stories to herself. Thanks for your e-mail and for having the sense to discontinue running along the crime-filled streets of Rome. (Aren't all large foreign cities crime-filled? I watch TV. I know.) It's probably evening there by now, so how was the Vatican? Did you see the pope?

PPS: Don't even bother writing again unless you describe what you're eating. Throw me a bone, for Pete's sake.

I closed my account, powered off, and scooped up Nora in my arms, holding her upside down on our way upstairs.

☙ ❧ ☙

"Work it, sisters," Laura ordered as we did a set of twenty crunches on the grass outside the public library. She paced among our curled bodies and adjacent strollers. "You get as much as you give, ladies. How much do you want?"

"Shut up," I heard one woman say under her breath. I snorted on my exhale. My abs, so long buried beneath the trauma of childbearing, were awakening like a hungry bear in spring. Their complaints were loud and obnoxious and not at all helping me "work it."

We finished the set and lay on our backs, not ashamed to moan. If pushing a cantaloupe through an opening the size of a McDonald's straw had taught us anything, it was that dignity was a thing of the past. Making inappropriate sounds on the library lawn was the least of our problems.

I rolled over and pushed myself to a sitting position. "I think I may have to resort to surgical help," I said to Kylie.

She gripped her stroller to help herself to a standing position. "Nonsense," she said, tucking a wayward strand of hair under her ball cap. "You're beautiful, inside and out. Don't you dare buy into the idea that a woman is her waist size. You're much more than that." She steered her stroller alongside mine as the group commenced its walk.

Our path cut through and around Main Street that morning, which meant there were plenty of distractions for stroller passengers but also that we were only able to walk down the middle of the street in order to accommodate all the members of our parade. We spent a lot of time avoiding being hit by oncoming traffic, but by the looks of Laura's set jaw and determined gait, we weren't going to let a few disgruntled drivers slow us down. I could just hear the lecture one of them would get should he challenge our leader's route:

"Thank you for your concern, Mr. Schmitt, but did you read the recent report on obesity issued by the governor's council? It's really very persuasive, particularly the section about giving up the

use of one's motor vehicle in favor of a bicycle or walking as modes
of personal transportation."

Poor Mr. Schmitt would slink back to his gas-guzzling,
fat-padding motor vehicle, never again to make the mistake of
taking on the Strut-n-Strollers.

"I know it's difficult to feel beautiful when you walk by
fashion magazines and feel nothing in common with the
models on the covers," Kylie said, her head bobbing up and
down as she walked.

"I've gotta tell you, Kylie," I said, tossing Nora's empty
juice box into a black trash bin, "this is interesting to hear
coming from a Solomon's Closet representative. Don't you
guys sell beauty products?"

"Oh, no," she said, bristling. "We offer *lifestyle* products.
Solomon's Closet is a Christian lingerie company."

I could feel her gauging my reaction. "Ahem. Christian
lingerie? I've never, eh, thought of lingerie as having a religious
preference."

She smiled. "Solomon's Closet is about women of the church
reclaiming what is rightfully theirs: a healthy sex life within
the parameters of marriage. So often we've been made to feel
that anything having to do with our sexual selves is dirty and
should be suppressed. But Solomon's Closet works to change
that, to enlighten women of faith to become who they were
created to be." She tilted her chin heavenward in allegiance to
her mission. "Solomon's Closet products are designed to help a
woman showcase her unique beauty, not cover it up. We want
women to *be* themselves, not *hide* themselves."

I'll bet, I thought. If there's one place it's difficult to hide,
it's in a black lace teddy.

We walked in silence, my head battling out how to make sense of Kylie. Stable Woman With Good Self-Image Who Happens To Sell Lingerie was in a dead heat with Brainwashed QVC Wannabe Giving Party Line To Prospective Bait.

"So is Solomon's Closet like other home-based gigs? Hosting parties, recruiting your friends, all that?"

"Yes, we do work within that model," Kylie said, slowing to give Brenna her pacifier. Brenna was having nothing of it. In fact, judging by her violent reaction, I was guessing Brenna hadn't taken a pacifier in a while. She started to thrash as she cried. Kylie was getting frantic. She rummaged around in the stroller carriage for another decoy. "We've found women to be most comfortable in their homes, particularly with lingerie," she said over Brenna's screams. I was impressed with her cool voice in the face of infant distress. "The parties are great fun, actually, once everyone gets over their initial shyness." Having found her thumb, Brenna was quiet and Kylie sighed with relief. "Lourdes didn't say anything about thumb sucking," she muttered, tossing the pacifier in the stroller basket.

I wanted to ask who Lourdes was and how she knew about Brenna's self-soothing habits, but I didn't have the chance. Laura Ingalls barked at us to pick up the pace. I tried to picture her at a Solomon's Closet party and felt the hair on the back of my neck stand on end.

"Mommy," Nora said from her cubby under the stroller canopy. "What's my name?"

"I can't remember. Trixie?"

"No," she said, giggling.

"Gertrude?"

"No, silly."

"I know. How about Helga?"

Nora gasped through her giggles. "No, Mommy. My name is *Nora*. Nora Hope Henry Elliott."

"Henry?"

She nodded. "That's my baby brother's name."

Kylie caught her breath and stared at my midriff. "Are you expecting, Heidi? Congratulations! That's so exciting."

I shook my head in protest. "No, actually, I'm not pregnant. Nora's just become vocal about her wishes for siblings." I tried shooting Nora my censor glare, but as with her father, it had absolutely no impact.

"Well," Kylie said, arching lightly penciled eyebrows under the bill of her cap, "it sounds like it's at least being discussed. And if that's the case, you should think about coming to my house tomorrow night. I'm having a Solomon's Closet get-together and I think you'd be interested in what I have to say." She smiled. "I've worked with many women over the years who got involved with the business while pregnant. It seems to be the perfect time to look for a professional outlet to help with growing family expenses."

My hand went to my belly. "Really? Pregnant women don't think it's too much to handle?" And people bought lingerie from women shaped like Boohbahs?

"It works out perfectly," said Kylie. "Solomon's Closet is designed in a way that lets you be your own boss and work at your own pace. You do as much or as little as you want."

This woman was sucking me in. "Tomorrow night, you say?"

Kylie produced a business card out of nowhere and forked it over. "Seven o'clock. Here's all my contact information and my home address. It will be casual, relaxing, informative. No pressure, I promise. Just come with an open mind and an empty stomach." She winked. "Like I said, Solomon's Closet is all about women enjoying life to its fullest, and that includes dessert."

I tucked her card into my jacket pocket. "I'll think about it," I said. "Thanks for the invitation."

"You're welcome," Kylie said as she rearranged Brenna's gingham hat to shade her from the late-morning sun. "Just as fair warning, though, Heidi. This meeting could change your life." She tilted her head and smiled at me, her eyes shining in the sunshine. I felt like I was watching the end of a really great infomercial.

I forced my own eyes to stay trained on her face instead of rolling to the back of my head. My mouth pulled itself into a smile. "Consider me warned."

ℰ 𝔻 ℰ

For my fifth birthday, my parents hired a clown. I remember being herded to the middle of our backyard, chin itching with the elastic of my purple birthday hat. I sat clustered with my preschool and neighborhood buddies. I'm sure adults hovered around the periphery, but the only one I cared about was our hired clown, Binkie, self-proclaimed Goofiest Guy At The Party. Binkie wore baggy red and yellow polka-dot pants and golf shoes caked in gold glitter. Blue suspenders were covered in buttons, many of them free tokens from political elections. Strange bedfellows blanketed Binkie's shirt: Richard Nixon smiled just above Jimmy Carter. "Teachers Vote Democrat!"

sat right next to a blinking outline of a Republican elephant. Newly elected Ronald Reagan held the majority of suspender real estate, his movie star smile promising the end of big government.

What riveted the eyes of ten five-year-olds, however, was the makeup. Clowns on television, clowns in our coloring books, clowns on animal cracker packaging—none of these sweated. But Binkie sweated. It was a particularly warm May afternoon, and the rest of us nonclowns were dressed in shorts and T-shirts. I wore my new Smurfette tank top over white shorts with blue trim. Binkie should have been so lucky. The polka-dot pants didn't breathe, and his rainbow nylon Afro baked in the afternoon sunlight. Under the wild curls, a blanket of white stage makeup slowly melted and ran down Binkie's face. The white bled into purple stars drawn on Binkie's cheeks and then into the exaggerated red mouth. When he tried to dab the rivulets off his face, the river became even muddier and Binkie's pasty skin surfaced in sickly gray blotches.

I was transfixed, and not with Binkie's disappearing scarves and popping balloons. I had to bite my lip to keep from crying when he pulled me to the front and led the crowd in "Happy Birthday." By that time, his eyeliner had smudged into dark circles around his eyes and I had to focus on my mom's face at the back of the group to keep control. When she asked me later what I'd thought, I'd shrugged and said, "His face was gross." My mother took this as a sign of ungratefulness and sulked the rest of the afternoon. And despite the promise of trapeze artists, elephants, and the tightrope, I'd never been able to risk a trip to the circus, even into adulthood.

So it was with this harrowing memory that I decided on a

no-clown theme for Nora's fourth birthday party. I stood with her in the party aisle at Target, perusing our choices.

"How about Dora?"

"I love Dora!"

"Great," I said, grabbing a paper tablecloth, plates, and napkins.

"No, I want princesses."

I unloaded Dora and reached for pink. "Okay. Let's go, peanut. We have more shopping to do."

"No, no, no," Nora said, pulling princess napkins out of my hand. "I want Blue's Clues."

I took a deep breath. "Fine. Blue it is. Now let's move it."

I heard a woman chuckling to herself. I turned.

She shook her head. "Isn't it pathetic?" she said. "The selection is so *dismal.* I've tried many times to convince myself to go the Target route." She gestured toward the stacked shelves. "But every time I get here, I just can't bear the thought of my Harrison having a carbon-copy birthday party. It's just so . . . *sad.*"

I stared at her, unblinking. She didn't appear to need me to respond, so I didn't.

"This year," she said, "I think we're doing pirates. Maybe start out with brunch at our house mid morning and have the actors arrive around eleven. We used the same troupe last year for my daughter's *Titanic* sweet sixteen, and they're just marvelous. They'll set up a portable moat for the pirate theme. Harry's turning seven. Is that about how old she is?" She pointed a French-tip acrylic at Nora. "Boys are harder than girls because of the video games. Such high expectations for the visual element. Though girls are harder to pin down for the invitation list." She reached up and cleaned the shelf of kid-size gift bags and curly adhesive ribbons. She turned to go, saying over her shoulder as she left, "Good luck!"

"Thanks," I muttered and wished for a place to sit down.

"Mommy, I want Nemo."

I nodded mutely, exchanged Blue for the fish, and lifted Nora into the cart. We pushed out of the party aisle and toward toddler fashions, where, for $9.99, I would buy a carbon-copy pair of jeans for my pathetic birthday girl.

℮ ℈ ℮

"Can you believe that?" I said to Willow over the phone an hour later. "She's hiring a troupe. And setting up a moat."

"This seems to be a trend," Willow said. I could hear The Loft's milk steamer screeching in the background. "I have clients who spend more on their kids' birthday parties than on a limited edition Rothko."

"Nora," I called to the backseat. "Turn it down a notch."

She stopped her shout-sing of "If You're Happy and You Know It." "Sorry, Mom. I can't help it."

"Do your best."

She commenced singing at a normal volume.

"Tell me some other humdingers," I said. "What are the nouveaux riches doing for the wee ones' birthdays these days?"

"Once a client told me she'd flown ten of her daughter's friends to New York to see the musical *Annie*. The little girl was turning ten, the same age as the red-headed heroine, you might remember."

"You're kidding."

"My favorite, though, was the couple who rented out pairs of wild animals from the zoo for their son's fourth birthday. A kind of twisted Noah's Ark theme, without the worldwide destruction. Two iguanas, two chinchillas, even two zebras. But," she said and had to stifle a giggle to finish her story, "the howler monkeys scared the kids so much they had to cut the party short, even before the camel rides."

"You are lying to me. That's against one of the Big Ten, you know."

"I am entirely serious," she said, chuckling. "So pirates and moats are nothing. What's the plan for Nora's fourth? Did you want me to help with the caviar order? I have connections."

"Yes, please," I said, pulling into our driveway. "I think Russian, don't you? It's so well-paired with little smokies, juice boxes, and Nemo noisemakers."

Nora was trying to escape from her car seat. Poor thing had no idea she'd be harnessed to one of those until her wisdom teeth were removed. "Mommy," she said, "I want out." She began to whimper.

"I'll call you later, Willow," I said. "Mutiny in the Civic."

"Thanks for calling," she said. "I'll check on the caviar, but isn't that a conflict of interest? Fish eggs at a Nemo party?"

"Sick," I said, clicking my phone shut and opening Nora's door to rescue the damsel in distress.

chapter/nine

"He's here!" Nora ran, arms pumping, to the front door and heaved it open.

"Hey, squirt." Nora's favorite babysitter, Micah, stood in the doorway and ruffled her hair. "Cool outfit."

"Thank you," Nora said coyly. She turned slowly so we could fully grasp the beauty of a baggy dark blue unitard I'm ashamed to own. Yoga phase, late nineties. Nora had accessorized with a feather boa, which she'd crossed around her torso like a round of ammunition. Jake's Twins cap sat backwards on her head.

"Come in, Micah," I said, pulling Claudia Schiffer out of the way. "How are you doing?"

"Fine. Tired. Our gig ran really late last night." Micah had little success hiding the pride in his voice.

"Traumatic Static really taking off, then?" I asked, holding back a smile. Micah had been a student of mine when I taught Spanish at the high school. He was an unruly but surprisingly sweet sophomore at the time, and I'd come to have great fondness for this boy and all his piercings. He'd gotten the highest grade in my class, though he would have died before making it public knowledge. And I'd seen the sweet way he looked after his three younger siblings. Micah had been surprised when I'd asked him to sit for Nora, but they'd become best buds.

"We were at The Dive. You know the bar on Highlands?"

I tugged on the strap of my slingback. "I know *of* it. I don't frequent it." I cocked my head and brought out the teacher voice. "Besides, you're only nineteen. How did you get in?"

He smirked. "Musician's privileges, *señora*. Don't worry. I'm not into the juice, anyway. I was there for the music." His face had become serious, one that any student of Iggy Pop would love.

"Good to hear," I said, standing and smoothing my skirt. "You're too bright to waste time getting sloshed at The Dive."

"You're dressed up," he said. It was my turn for outfit appraisal.

"I'm going to a party in Avalon."

"Nice," Micah said, nodding with appreciation. Nora had brought him markers and a pad of paper. He sat with her at the kitchen table. "There are some monstrous houses in that neighborhood."

"Exactly. Do I look the part?" I was wearing a black and white polka-dot skirt that flared just above the knee. The shirt was a matching black, with three-quarter-length sleeves and a V-neck, all tricks of the postpartum trade.

My audience gave me the once-over. Getting a fashion report from a garage-band bass player and my boa-clad daughter was not my first choice, but Jake had already left for his poker night.

Nora scrunched up her nose. "I like pink."

Micah shrugged. "It works."

Good enough. "Thanks, you two." I grabbed my purse. "Nora, bedtime in a half hour. Micah, eat whatever you can find that doesn't violate expiration dates."

They waved, markers in hand, and I pulled the door shut behind me.

℮ ℈ ℮

Kylie's house was in Springdale's only gated community. When developers had proposed building Avalon Estates on the north side of town, we commoners had reacted with envy only lightly masked by disdain. We'd watched from afar as the city council approved the project and construction began. One by one, gargantuan homes rose from sprawling foundations, their huge imprints dotting the freshly developed hillsides. No two houses were alike, as the clientele in this target market were looking for individualized displays of outrageous wealth. Some people preferred Asian marble, for example, rather than Tuscan or Greek. English rather than French-inspired land-scaping. You get the idea.

When Kylie called with directions, she told me they'd recently moved into 11 Ridgecrest Boulevard, a sprawling home roughly the size of Uzbekistan. Thousands of char-coal-colored bricks piled on top of each other to enclose a six-bedroom, eight-bath little charmer. The only time I'd been allowed entrance into Avalon was when I'd tagged along with a realtor friend checking on a listing. I'd seen a printout on the Zimmerman house at that time and remembered the stats. A girl doesn't easily forget the words *eight-bath*.

Kylie met me at two massive front doors painted the color of Merlot. I'd been unable to reach the brass knockers on the twin fifteen-footers, so I'd settled on ringing the doorbell and waiting between topiaries that arched on both sides of the entrance.

"Heidi," Kylie said. "Welcome." She wore a long tailored jacket made of pale blue silk. The brown embroidery matched her eyes. She stepped aside and allowed me to pass. "Excuse the mess. We're still getting settled."

I hope I mumbled something socially appropriate, but I can't be sure. I should have just asked for a moment to compose myself because what I saw took my breath away.

The foyer of Kylie's home rose three stories and was cut down the middle with a sweeping staircase. The floor was a deep gray marble with black veins, classy enough to be an attraction on its own but not so pushy as to overshadow the vibrant rugs that covered it. The feel of the space was modern and indulgent. I'd like to say it was comfortable and livable, but I don't think that's what the architect was going for.

I'm sure there was artwork and probably a smattering of artifacts from Tut's tomb, but I couldn't keep my eyes off the ceiling. Kylie followed my gaze.

"It's a Tabuchi," she said. "I guess he's a famous glass artist from Tokyo, and the original owners commissioned the piece." The "piece" formed a suspended oval twenty feet up. Mr. Tabuchi had created a three-dimensional ocean of glass. Abstract, delicate waves in blues, greens, silver, and white swirled above our heads, catching the evening light coming from a rotunda of windows in the dome overhead.

Kylie put her arm around my shoulders and steered me to the right. "It's interesting," she said, since I had gone mute, "but not really our style. If you know anyone who'd be interested, we'll be selling it this fall."

Sure thing. I had a *list* of potential buyers. My pastor,

for one. The homeless man who slept in the IHOP parking lot . . .

Kylie led me into what I would have affectionately referred to as the parlor, were I the mistress of the manor. I wasn't really sure what one did in a parlor, but perhaps it had something to do with serving dessert and lots of champagne. The room was spacious but not cavernous and infused with the smells of dark chocolate, imported coffee, and spring flowers. The walls were covered in striped cream wallpaper that appeared to be woven in silk. I was positive it had not come from Jake's store as a buy-one-get-a-matching-border-half-off deal. The room was big enough to be divided into two seating sections. Chairs and couches were covered in complementary greens and rose, and judging by the spring-themed artwork and decor, it was likely the furniture would change with the season. That was one of the nice things about cream silk wallpaper—so versatile.

For the event, all seats faced the middle of the room, where there stood a round table covered with flowers and Solomon's Closet products. Different heights of vases peppered the table-top, along with flickering candles and bottles of body lotions and sprays. Mannequins were set up to display the spring line. "Mannequin" is being generous. They were more like half mannequins, stopping at midthigh, but Solomon's Closet mannequins didn't need a lot of real estate. Loose peony blossoms wove in and out of polka-dot panties. Tea lights in turquoise glass holders made the light dance on clusters of nighties and robes.

"Mallory," Kylie said, pulling a blonde woman in a black wraparound dress away from a circle of conversation and toward us. "This is Heidi Elliott. She's my guest tonight."

Mallory had beautiful teeth. "Hello, Heidi. It's a pleasure."

I shook her hand. "Nice to meet you, Mallory." I smiled in return and wished I'd worn my retainers like I'd been told.

"Mallory, Heidi also has a three-year-old."

Mallory lit up like a firecracker. "Fantaaastic!" she said. "My son, Julian, turned three in February. What's your child's name?"

"Nora," I said. "She turns four this month."

"Eeehxcellent!" Mallory said, nodding enthusiastically. "Nora. What a sweet name. We're on the lookout for girl names." She patted her stomach.

"Mallory's expecting her second," Kylie said victoriously. She widened her eyes to remind me I wanted that, too.

"Congratulations," I said sincerely. "How far along are you?"

"Five months," she said, and I tried to remember I loved Jesus and shouldn't hate. Mallory's five-month-along stomach was the depth of a flat-screen TV. Love neighbor as self, love neighbor as self.

"We'll be getting started in a few minutes, Heidi, if you'd like to stop by the dessert tables before we sit down." She gave Mallory a pat on the tummy before leaving to mingle.

I bid farewell to Skinny and headed toward the food. Tables on each end of the room were set with bouquets of tulips and hydrangeas. The desserts didn't look too bad either. I had to skip the brut, as I was hoping to find myself with child within the week, but I settled for a piece of carrot cake and a cookie involving chunks of Lindt chocolate and found an empty chair.

From my vantage point, everyone in the group of twenty or so looked to be avoiding the sleazy salesperson image. No gold medallions, no suitcases bursting with dusty merchandise, no loud laughing and business-card swapping. Kylie had said there would be a mix of seasoned consultants and newbies like myself. I tried sorting the women into those two groups as I munched on my carrot cake.

"Thank you for coming," Kylie said as people quieted and settled in their seats. "It is my pleasure to welcome you to my home for the first time since our move."

The women around me nodded their approval, everyone all smiles for Kylie and her humble digs. Out of the corner of my eye, I saw a man slip into the room from a side door. Tall, athletic build, salt and pepper hair that looked like it had a standing appointment with a trend-savvy stylist. He caught me looking at him and smiled, revealing white teeth and tiny wrinkles around cornflower blue eyes. I smiled quickly and turned back toward Kylie.

"This is the day," she said, back straight and hands open before her. "Ladies, this is the day that could change your life forever."

About half the women in the room were murmuring like they were at a tent meeting.

"We have some valued guests here with us tonight," Kylie said, letting her gaze linger as she eyed the group. "If this is your first up-close-and-personal meeting with Solomon's Closet, you're in for a treat. You have been invited by someone who cares about you, treasures your friendship, and wants the very best for you."

Heads were nodding. Some of the women reached over to

their guests and patted a knee or squeezed a hand. Since I was the valued guest of the orator, I was free to glance around the room without having to reciprocate a pat. I paid particular attention to the women wearing little turquoise and brown pins in the shape of a star. These appeared to be the experienced Solomon's Closeters. They represented a variety of races and ages but had one thing in common: They looked very put together. Coiffures were shaped and well cut. Makeup was simple and pretty. Smiles were wide and flossed. I wouldn't go as far as Stepford, but there were similarities. The verdict was still out as to whether this sheen was authentic or creepy.

"If you get nothing else out of tonight," Kylie said, "take home with you the fact that you are gifted, you are worthy, and you are beautiful."

"Mmmm," agreed the pin wearers, some of them closing their eyes to bask in those truths. I started fidgeting and was getting a preliminary read on the nearest exits.

"What makes Solomon's Closet different from other businesses?" Kylie asked. She made her way slowly around the periphery of the round table, taking time to make eye contact with her audience. "Solomon's Closet allows women autonomy. Self-direction. Power. The opportunity to build relationships. And most importantly . . ." Kylie had stopped and was laying a hand on pregnant Mallory's shoulder. "Ladies, Solomon's Closet allows a woman to spend precious time with her family." There was such wattage behind Mallory's grin, I thought she'd jump up, fake belly and all, and lead us in "We Are Family."

I felt under my chair for my purse and was prepared to fake an emergency phone call as my exit cue when Kylie looked straight at me and said, "But let's cut to the chase, shall we?"

Yes, please, I thought. Chase cutting is much more up my alley.

"Imagine with me, if you will, that we are not on Ridgecrest Boulevard in Avalon Estates. Imagine we are not in Springdale but are instead in south Chicago in a tiny one-bedroom apartment with little heat in the winter and jungle humidity in the summer. Imagine the little girl who lives there with a mother she rarely sees because that mother is working so hard to support the girl and her two brothers that she has no time to spend with those she loves. There is no father in this scenario. He left long ago without even a good-bye and hasn't been heard of since."

Kylie took a deep breath. "This girl lives in the richest nation in the world, but you'd never know it. She wears clothes with holes, though they are clean. Her hair is outgrown and her face is drawn, but she stays in school, even through the jeering in junior high and the isolation of high school. This girl works two jobs as soon as she is of age, cleaning toilets, flipping burgers, pushing brooms — anything to help feed her family and survive another month's rent."

The room was quiet. All this talk about cleaning toilets was putting a different light on the opulence around us. I, for one, didn't think the chocolate was as tasty as it had been a few minutes ago. I put down my cookie and waited for Kylie to continue.

"The girl finishes high school, an enormous accomplishment in her family and one that is a source of pride for her mother for the rest of her life." Kylie swallowed before continuing. "The girl works double shifts to pay for classes at the community college. During one of those classes, she meets her future husband, a man who dreams big and convinces the girl to dream right along with him. Soon they marry."

She stopped, her eyes lingering on the man in the back. Kylie returned her gaze to the group and smiled. "Ten years and two children later, the man and his bride move into a beautiful home at 11 Ridgecrest Boulevard in Avalon Estates."

I was too cool to gasp like the other girls, but I thought about it.

"This," Kylie said, gesturing to the silk wallpaper, the vaulted ceilings, the tables laden with flowers and chocolate, "this, ladies, is the product of a dream. And to you I say only this: Dream big."

The room erupted in applause. Several of the women near me were sniffing and wiping their eyes, and I must say there was a lump in my throat, too. I mean, come on. South side of Chicago?

At this, Kylie introduced another Solomon's Closet consultant, a woman named Tarin who had skin the color of cinnamon. She distributed glossy brochures outlining the Solomon's Closet mission statement. We rode right along down the current, as we were told our families would thank us for the extra time we had with them and for the money we'd contribute to the household income. Tarin walked us through the basic principles of the business, emphasizing heavily the no-risk premise of coming on board. While we'd be required to make a small down payment to cover start-up costs, that money would quickly be returned to us after recouping the funds through sales.

Tarin talked for about ten minutes and then the party

adjourned with an admonition from Kylie to take our time checking out the products on the round table and to ask anyone with a star pin should we have any questions.

I was looking at a pink bra called the Twin Fawns Brassiere when Kylie put her arm around my shoulders.

"Thanks for coming," she said, smiling warmly.

"My pleasure," I said, putting the bra back into its niche next to an iris. "You have quite the story."

She nodded. "Solomon's Closet really gave me and Russ the life we wanted. We believe in the product, so sharing it with others isn't difficult. It just makes sense."

I had the feeling a lot of things would make more sense if one pondered them on Tuscan marble.

"Heidi," Kylie said, steering me to the periphery of the room, "I want you to know I am in no way pressuring you to make a decision about this tonight." She waved to someone who was leaving and spoke to me in hushed tones. "But if you are at all interested in joining the Solomon's Closet team, as my guest this evening, you'll pay no start-up fee." She looked me in the eye. "From what you've told me, I think this would be a great fit for you and your family. You could continue staying home. You could have another baby without worrying about what it would mean for your finances. Plus, your husband would probably appreciate your financial contribution."

My husband would probably most appreciate the Twin Fawns. "I'm not a very good salesperson," I said, shaking my head.

"I can hardly believe that," Kylie said too loudly and then checked her volume. "Really, I disagree," she said more softly. "You are dynamic, beautiful, and a woman who has confidence in herself."

"Thank you," I said, though how in the world would she know that? Did I exude confidence and beauty at Strut-n-Stroll?

"Solomon's Closet is a bit, shall we say, unorthodox," Kylie said. "Not everyone can understand pairing faith with lingerie."

I thought again of Laura Ingalls and winced.

"But I believe in what we do and what we are selling. Women, especially Christian women, *deserve* to feel beautiful, for themselves and for their husbands. Don't you agree?"

"Well, yes, but—"

Kylie took my hands in hers. "Like I said, there is no pressure here. Why don't you take some time to think about it and get back to me when you've made a decision."

I raised my eyebrows in surprise. I thought all sales types went in for the kill and wouldn't let you out of their clutches until you'd sold a soul or two. Giving me time to think, eh? A point in Solomon's Closet's favor. "That sounds good. I should talk this over with Jake."

"Absolutely," Kylie said, nodding slowly. "This is a family decision. Though I must say," she said, voice lowered, "I have never, in ten years of working with Solomon's Closet, had a husband say no to his wife selling lingerie." She laughed at her own joke.

"Boys will be boys," I offered feebly.

"Exactly," she said, clapping her hands together. "We've built a business around that fact. And," she added hastily, her tone suddenly demure, "around our conviction that Christians need to take back the true meaning of a healthy sexual relationship."

"Right," I said. "I'll give it some thought. You have a lovely home, Kylie. Thanks for the invitation."

"I'll see you at Strut-n-Stroll, if not sooner." She smiled, gave me a prissy I'm-not-really-touching-you hug, and walked back to the center table.

On the way out, I took one more look at the Tabuchi and wondered how I knew I'd be back.

chapter/ten

"Nora, leave the fishies in the bowl. Fish need water, sweetie. You don't want Nemo to die, do you?"

Nora stopped midswoop with the green mini fishnet. "You mean like when Scar kills Mufasa in *The Lion King*?" Her eyes were large and mournful.

"Kind of, only with less violence," I said, taking the net out of her hand. "Why don't you go outside and play on your swing set while we wait for your friends?"

I was starting to wish one could throw a birthday party for four-year-olds without actually inviting any. Nora had "helped" set the table with Nemo-ware, except that she'd wanted to keep all the plates for herself and use our china instead. Then she'd "helped" put a cup of jelly beans by each plate, except that she'd eaten half the bag and run out before finishing. Extracting the party favors from their natural habitat and forcing them to flop around on the floor was the last straw. Nora needed some preparty alone time.

"Mommy," she whined as I led her to the back door and opened the screen. "I'm waiting for my friends. Today's my birfday party."

"I know, honey," I said. "They'll be here soon. I'll call you as soon as they arrive."

She trudged out to her swing set, her hoop skirt dragging on the grass. Today's ensemble was bride meets Elmo. Nora was wearing a flower girl dress from the late seventies that I'd seen hanging on the end of a rack at a garage sale. I'd crossed over two lanes of traffic to nab it, and Nora had rewarded me with near delirium, she was so happy. Over the worn pink bodice she'd donned a red shrug in a material that could have been shorn from Elmo himself. Fluffy spikes of synthetic fur rustled as she climbed up the ladder to her small slide.

I smiled as I turned back inside, ready to finish the prep work for the party. I looked at my watch.

"Jake," I called down to the basement office. "Nora needs a playmate while I finish up."

"M'kay," he said, distraction written all over his voice. A few minutes passed with no sign of the husband.

"Jake!"

"Coming," he said. I could hear the printer going like mad. Jake came bounding up the stairs and into the kitchen. A playful smile danced on his lips. "How about Burma?"

I rolled my eyes. "Let's hear it."

Jake's eyes were wide. "Six nights, food included, airfare, and lodging for five ninety-nine a person." He flicked the printout in his hand for emphasis. "Unbelievable."

I shook my head and sighed. Jake nurtured a strange obsession with Internet travel deals. This interest, though quietly present before we had Nora, had mushroomed into a full-blown fixation after her birth. At all hours of the day and night, he'd rise like a bleary-eyed phoenix from the basement and proclaim the latest hot deal.

"Istanbul for six fifty a person, Heids!"

"Orlando, Disney included, for four seventy-five a person!"

"Woo-hoo! Three nights in a four-star Vegas hotel for three hundred bones, baby!"

Initially, I'd waded into the waters with him, watching him search his favorite sites and getting sucked into a picture of myself on a beach in the Virgin Islands, watching Nora romp in the sapphire ocean while Jake acted as my own private cabana boy. The problem was that every scenario ended in The Catch. "Travel must be completed in the next seventy-two hours," for example. "Airport taxes in the sum of seven thousand dollars not included." "Hotel cannot guarantee space upon arrival, though cots are allowed in the lobby." You get the picture.

I had a theory that scavenging for the fastest and cheapest way to St. Lucia was Jake's way of feeling unfettered. The indulgence of an escape route from the confines of the store, parental responsibility, and yard work. A delicious alternative to worrying about certified letters and past-due electric bills. All hypothetically speaking, thus far.

I shook my head at the Burma deal. "Let's talk about it after the party, okay?"

Jake stashed the paper on top of the fridge and opened the door to the backyard, singing a few bars of "Kokomo" on his way out. I resisted the urge to put the Burma printout in the trash, knowing the fine print would surface within a day anyway.

The stove clock read five minutes until go-time. I took stock of party readiness. Our dining room was decked out in blue and orange twisted streamers. A cluster of helium balloons emblazoned with Nemo's face floated in the corner. The table was set for cake and ice cream, and most of the kids were getting jelly beans. The unlucky few were stuck with peanuts and raisins due to Nora's indiscretions. I didn't feel too sorry for the raisin children, though, as sugar was going to be the theme for the day and would leave no child unwired. It would have been faster to just forgo the chewing and inject it intravenously, but after cake, ice cream, candy, and juice boxes, the parents of these children would probably not be asking me to administer any medical treatments to their offspring.

I was sweeping the kitchen when the phone rang. "Hello?" I answered. The line was broken up by static. "Hello?" I said again.

"Heidi! Hello!"

"Annie!" I said, my heart jumping. "I can't believe it's you! Is everything okay?"

"Everything's great," she said. It sounded like she was standing inside a diesel engine. "I'm sorry if the connection's not so hot. I'm calling from a public phone right outside Vatican City. The traffic here is—" The rest of her sentence was drowned out by a mufflerless bus that must have eaten her.

"Annie? Can't hear you. Stop talking until that bus spits you out."

"—but I loved Rome so much I decided to stay another week. What did you say? I couldn't hear you."

"Nothing," I said. "I have so many questions I don't know where to start."

"Heids, I'm sorry I haven't been as consistent with e-mail as I should be. I just get so busy during the day, and by the time I have a chance to write at night, I collapse in my *osteria*."

"Right," I said. "We call it a pillowtop here, but I know what you mean."

She laughed, though with the time delay it sounded like she was part of the studio audience. "How's the birthday girl? I can't believe she's turning four."

The doorbell rang and I peeked around the corner to see Lori and Olivia through the front screen door. I waved them in. "Nora's great. We're just about to start our Nemo party."

The line was crackling again. "Your Janet Reno party?"

"Nemo," I corrected. I mouthed "sorry" to Lori, who waved me away. "Annie, I hate to do this, but I really need to go. Our guests are arriving and I need to get Nora from the backyard."

"No problem," Annie said, and I thought I heard a false chipper note in her voice. "Can I talk with Norie before we hang up?"

"Absolutely. I miss you and love you, Annie. E-mail me more often or I'll start a vicious rumor involving you and a Sicilian crime ring."

She laughed. "Love you, too. Have fun with Janet Reno."

"Nora," I called into the yard. "Auntie Annie is on the phone. She wants to talk with the birthday girl."

Jake helped Nora scramble off the swing and she came running. Four steps from the door, she tripped on the hem of her dress and went sprawling on the pavement. I dropped the phone on the linoleum and ran to her.

"Mommy," she wailed, staring through crocodile tears at the blood that was pooling on both knees and the palms of her hands. "I have owwwwwieees."

Jake hurried over from the swing set but I got there first. I scooped her up in my arms and walked slowly to the back door and the kitchen. "Do you want to say hi to Annie?" I asked Nora. Her arms were wound tightly around my neck.

She shook her head and began another round of weeping.

"Annie," I said into the phone, loudly enough to be heard above Nora's sobs, "Nora fell down and I need to help her. Can you call back later?"

"Maybe not today but I will soon," she said. "Tell her I love her and happy birthday. Poor thing." A motorcycle swallowed her next words but I assumed it was some sort of good-bye.

"Love you," I said and hung up. I turned to Lori, who stood with Olivia. "Sorry about that. Best friend calling from Italy."

The doorbell rang again. "I'll get it," said Lori. "Come on, Livi." Olivia allowed herself to be guided by her mom, though she walked sideways to enable one last look at the carnage.

"Let's clean you up," I said to Nora, who by now had made a decrescendo to whimpering. We walked to the bathroom and I washed out her scrapes, trying my best not to incur more pain. Five minutes later, Neosporined and bandaged, Nora let me help her down from the bathroom counter and hobbled back to her party.

We rounded the corner from the hallway and were greeted by a cheery group of moms, dads, and corresponding offspring. In addition to Lori and Olivia, I'd called four other neighborhood families with kids roughly Nora's age. Emily and Matt Smythe were there with their eighteen-month-old daughter, Lily, and their four-year-old, Kenna. Shannon McDill held two-year-old Blake, who was intent on pulling the hair of

Emery, Daniela Santos's youngest. Daniela's husband, Raúl, was standing with Matt and Jake. The three were already in a quickly escalating debate about the virtues of soccer compared with the barbarism of football.

Daniela and Shannon helped me corral the kids to the backyard, where I'd set out different stations of kid-friendly distractions. The kids fanned out to tables holding bubbles, new coloring books and crayons, sidewalk chalk, and Play-Doh. Nora appeared to be recuperating well enough from her injuries to be bossing around her entourage.

"Thanks for having us, Heidi," Lori said when the moms had congregated between the bubbles and the chalk. "What a beautiful day to have a birthday party."

She was right. Nora's late May birthday could mean anywhere from temps in the midforties, rain, and even sleet one year to upper eighties and sweat-inducing. This particular Saturday morning was the most perfect Springdale got: midseventies, light breeze, no humidity, and a splattering of cottony clouds in a bright sky.

"Emery was born in December, so outdoor parties won't be an option," Daniela said. She handed her daughter a red teether and set her down on a blanket she'd laid on the grass. She turned to the circle of women. "What have you girls been up to? I feel like we're finally coming out of hiding after a winter of hibernating."

"Seriously," Lori said, finishing a sip of lemonade. "I fantasize about green grass all winter but it takes me by surprise every single spring."

I nodded. "I don't think I ever truly appreciated the liberation of spring until I was cooped up all winter with a child.

There were times, long about January, when I had to remind myself that it was unethical and illegal to hijack a plane headed for Bali, even if I thought it was in my child's best interest."

Emily shook her head. "I don't know how you do it, Heidi. I would be climbing the walls by noon if I stayed home full-time."

Lori laughed. "Who says she makes it to noon? I'll bet by nine some days you're ready to apply to McDonald's."

I tried to laugh. "I certainly have my moments." Looking around the circle, I realized Daniela and I were the only stay-at-homers in the group. Lori worked part-time as an interior designer, Emily worked four days a week in as a financial consultant, and Shannon did something involving mortgages. Daniela, who had worked for a marketing firm up until Emery was born, had shifted gears and was staying home full-time as of a few months ago.

Emily smiled at me. "I know how you feel. I've tried both—staying home full-time and working full-time. The best fit for me was to do a mix. I loved being home during my maternity leaves with both girls, but I couldn't wait to brush off the part of my brain that I used at work."

My mind expanded that visual and I easily pictured entire regions of my brain lying atrophied and moss-covered, much like the wreckage of the *Titanic*. Almost immediately, though, I felt guilty for underestimating the amount of brain power it took to build a home.

"I agree," Shannon said. "I honestly think I'm a better mom because I have an outlet."

"I'm more patient now that I work a few days a week," Lori said. "The other day, Olivia whined nonstop for over an hour. The baby had an ear infection and I normally would have been at my wit's end. But it was my day off from work, and I'd already had enough time away from home that week, so I could be more patient."

Daniela cleared her throat. "I'm really happy to be at home full-time," she offered meekly. "I wanted to do it for years and I'm so glad it finally worked out."

After a moment of silence I asked, "So you don't regret quitting?"

Daniela shook her head. "Not at all. I put in my time there and I loved my job. But it was time to do this. I knew it was the right choice. Plus," she added, "I think Emery is benefiting from my time with her in ways my other two didn't. It's all about the number of hours." She picked up Emery, who sat at her feet, reaching for her mom.

The working women exchanged glances.

"Well," Emily said, "It's great that you've found the right choice for your family. I just know my kids would *not* benefit from more time with their mom if I was feeling like a caged animal all the time."

Ouch. I didn't know whether to be offended or worried that she'd struck a nerve in my *Titanic* brain.

We were saved by the inattention of males. The dads had been the backyard police, officiating between bubble blowers and Play-Doh eaters. But the men had gotten distracted by our basketball hoop and were on their way to start a pick-up game. Before one shot had been fired, however, Kenna and Nora started screaming while Olivia stood between the two girls, stunned. The shock wore off in half a second and Olivia joined the other girls in their screams. I ran behind Lori to the scene and saw a welt the size of a dime on Livi's right cheek.

Bee sting.

"It's okay, sweetheart," Lori said as she lifted her. "Heidi, can we have some ice?"

Jake was already on his way inside, trailed by the other sheepish-looking males.

"How about some cake and ice cream?" I asked the group. The nonstung partygoers cheered and Olivia sniffled.

We helped the kids inside and took turns washing hands at the kitchen and bathroom sinks. Livi sat at the table on her mom's lap, picking gingerly at her raisins before I intervened and poured half of Nora's jelly beans into Olivia's cup. The drought was my daughter's doing, after all.

After a motley rendition of "Happy Birthday," Nora blew out her candles. We had only one incident during the last half hour of the party, involving a Nemo balloon and contraband scissors. I was happy to have included the "no gifts, please" suggestion on our invitations. Being nice to each other, parents included, seemed to have a ninety-minute limit when a roomful of preschoolers was involved. If Nora had ended up with a queen's treasure trove of gifts to boot, it could have gotten ugly.

The party favors were a big hit with the kids, though reactions varied among the parents. Olivia's smile at getting to take home her very own goldfish was particularly pathetic because she looked like she'd gotten a root canal as part of the festivities. Her little swollen cheek made her face lopsided, but the fish seemed to help. Each of the five fish taken home was christened Nemo, but Nora named her remaining fish Jonah. I was pleased God had crossed her mind in our humble festivities, even if His prophet's name was given to a fish that would probably die within forty-eight hours.

Two hours from the party's start, our house was nearly empty. We stood on the front porch and waved as Daniela and Raúl left, the last to gather their brood and depart. I closed the front door and turned to Nora, who was dancing to some internal birthday disco mix.

"Did you have fun?" I asked, putting my arm around Jake as we waited for the verdict.

"I really, really, *really* had fun. Can I have more ice cream?" Her pupils were dilated and she'd developed a nervous tic.

"Don't think so, peanut," Jake said, throwing her up in the air. "It's against birthday rules to eat more than one's age in pounds of sugar." Nora giggled as she flew to the ceiling.

I started wiping frosting off the rungs of our dining room chairs and let my mind drift to the conversation in the back yard. Maybe we were better mothers when we left the house to pursue our own interests and careers. Or maybe Daniela was right and numbers didn't lie. Maybe the sheer quantity of hours we spent with our children, no matter our emotional or professional state, was what mattered. Maybe home was where the heart was, no matter how we tried to couch it.

Nora's giggles turned to whining and I heard Jake trying to reason with our tired, overstimulated, newly four-year-old birthday girl. Frosting removed, I rose from my hands and knees and went for a mop and pail.

chapter/eleven

Three weeks later I still hadn't made a decision about Kylie. The beginning of June launched us into glorious weather, pool time, and weekend trips to the lake. Theoretically, summer would have been a perfect time to reflect, reassess my life, and give serious thought to personal and professional goals. Realistically, however, my days began and ended in a flurry of sunscreen, playdates, and park visits. Nora and I were happy as clams, just not advancing in our careers.

It wasn't that I hadn't been taking action with our financial situation. I had. I'd spent Sundays cutting coupons from the newspaper, a mind-numbing exercise that made me want to hurt myself. I forced myself to move the scissors around the dotted lines of a coupon for thirty-five cents off frozen waffles, reasoning that every little bit helped. Though categorically opposed to Hamburger Helper, I snipped the fifty-five-cent coupon anyway and vowed to reform my food snobbery. Armed with a sheaf of savings, I filed my coupons in a cute blue organizer held together with a striped elastic band, waved it under Jake's nose for emphasis and praise, and remembered to bring it along only once out of the next four trips to the grocery store.

Considering it took twenty-one repeated actions to form a habit, I was on mark to reap the benefits of coupon cutting by early 2015.

Apart from my rocky start with coupons, I was making a conscious effort to be content with the little things. The single most important part of this strategy was avoiding Target. If we needed toilet paper, I sent Jake. If I ran out of Clorox, Jake was my man. No more accidental spending, I vowed, acknowledging with a cringe that trips to pick up Armor All often, mysteriously, ended with a hundred dollars on the credit card.

Admitting one had a problem was the first step, and I was on my way to recovery. I'd relapsed a couple of times when I needed to buy something involving aesthetic sensibility and could not rely on Jake. Clorox, yes, but picking out a swimsuit for Nora? Goodness, no. A graduation gift for our pastor's daughter? A card, maybe, but not the gift. He might come home with a grin, clutching a CD of Styx's Greatest Hits. So I'd gone and, like an alcoholic faced with happy hour, I'd faltered and given in, coming home with a new wardrobe for Nora, two DVDs, and thirty dollars' worth of gardening supplies. Technically, these were all things we could use and would frequently. But did we *need* them? And did I really want to open up that discussion? I wasn't about to move to a Quonset hut and wear nothing but a loincloth, all in the name of living without excess.

I vowed anew to remember my coupons.

The turning point came one Friday afternoon. Nora and I had returned from Strut-n-Stroll, where I'd walked with Laura Ingalls since Kylie was away on business. For the record, talking about women achieving their dreams was far less painful than working out with Sergeant Legalism. I'd never walked with such violent fervor in my life. When we arrived home, I had to will my aching legs to walk in a straight line up our front path, cursing Ingalls Wilder the whole way.

"I'll bet she also looks forward to vaccinations and trips to the DOT," I muttered to myself as I hefted my quads up the porch stairs. Nora beat me to the door and raced to an alphabet puzzle as soon as we entered. After I'd taken a shower and dressed, I asked Nora if she wanted to water the porch flowers with me. I headed to the kitchen sink to fill the watering can.

"Of course, *Olga*." Nora raised her eyebrows at me for my cue.

I cleared my throat. "Shall vee get somezeen for you to vater vid, my dear?" I asked in what was intended to be a thick Russian accent. It was my lot in life to entertain.

Nora smiled. "Yes, Olga. In American, this is called a *watering can*." She held up her red can and spoke slowly for the second-language learner.

"Vatering can. Da, I zee." Olga was intended to be from Mother Russia but had been known to migrate to Austria, India, even France on occasion. Annie probably wished Olga had accompanied her to Europe to serve as a multilingual translator.

Nora handed me her watering can to fill up first.

"Zank you." I flipped up the faucet handle.

I screamed and Nora hit the floor like a Marine under fire. The faucet handle had flown off its base and was still in my hand, detached and useless. The water, however, thought that whole handle thing was overrated as it continued to shoot in a wild fountain arching to the ceiling.

"Turn it off, Olga!" Nora yelled from her place on the floor.

"I'm trying," I said, cupping my hand over part of the spray to get a look. If I squinted just right, I thought I could see a miniscule slip of metal that looked like it might rotate or depress and turn off Old Faithful. I tried in vain to push, pull, and otherwise manipulate the part, but I needed pliers.

"Norie, come with me," I said to my cowering child.

She gripped my hand and scurried with me to the garage. "Olga, that was scary. Are you ever scared in Russia?"

I was muttering to myself, rummaging through the toolbox.

"Olga?"

"Hmm?" Found 'em. I dragged Nora back through the garage side door and into the kitchen.

"Olga." Nora tugged at my shirt. "Are you ever scared in Russia?"

"Scared in Russia?" I looked at her, trying to register what on earth she was talking about. "Oh," I said in Olga-voice. "Da, da. I'm scared in Mudder Russia because of somezeen called zee KGB. You vill learn some udder time."

Seriously. I needed a hobby.

I used the pliers to grasp the metal thing and pushed down until the fountain slowed to a trickle and then to a stop.

"Good job, Olga!" Nora cheered.

"Zank you," I said, eyeing the faucet warily.

The front door creaked and I heard Jake call, "Anybody home?"

Nora ran out of the kitchen and toward the front door shouting, "Daddy, Daddy, Olga turned off the fountain!"

Jake rounded the corner, Nora in his arms. He took one look at me, sopping wet, holding pliers and the broken faucet handle and said, "Olga?"

I pushed a soggy strand of hair out of my eyes. "We knew

its days were numbered, but today was this baby's last." I pointed with my pliers. "We're talking geyser."

Jake put Nora down and walked to the sink. "How'd you get it to turn off?" He started poking around on the broken base.

"Jake, I wouldn't—"

Water erupted into Jake's face and he shouted, "Give me the pliers!"

He tried forcing the metal slip down and apparently didn't have the finesse of a woman because he ripped the thing right off. He stood back from the spray, pliers still clenched and holding the part.

"I'll call the plumber," I said, already moving to the phone.

"Wait," Jake said. "Don't call the plumber."

"What?" I said, shouting to be heard over the water. "Jake, you can't be serious."

"We don't need a plumber," he yelled, squinting to see the base through the eruption. "I can fix it."

I stood, mouth open and trying to invoke calm. "Nora," I said, "do you remember the story of Noah?"

Jake ignored me and flew to the garage, returning with man's greatest ally and woman's vilest enemy: duct tape.

"You have got to be kidding me," I said.

Nora and I sat on a kitchen chair, out of range of the water works, and watched as Jake rigged a stopping mechanism. Sometime after the ball of tape reached the diameter of a softball, he stepped back, eyed his work, and sighed with satisfaction.

"I knew we didn't need a plumber. That was no sweat."

I helped Nora off my lap and went to inspect Jake's work. The softball had, indeed, reduced the water's velocity from bullets in an automatic weapon to pinging trickle. Victory.

I reached over to the softball to try turning the water off completely.

"Don't," said Jake, giving me the straight arm. "I mean," he said more calmly, "it's fine just like that."

I looked at him. "It is?"

He nodded, relaxed the arm pinned against my shoulder. "Sure. I can't exactly turn it all the way off. Not yet, anyway. We'll just leave it until I have some more time to work on it."

I looked at Jake, looked at the trickle. The stream would be perfect for rinsing off individual grains of salt. "Please let me call a plumber."

"No way," he shook his head. "I can figure this out on my own, without paying sixty bucks an hour plus parts. We just won't use it tonight. How about we call in pizza?" He started riffling through some papers by the phone. "Don't we have a coupon for pizza?"

I stood long enough to hear Jake mutter at a coupon he clutched in his hand, "Two mediums for nine ninety-nine? What a rip-off!"

Nora looked up at me and shook her head slowly. "Olga, Daddy's talking to himself."

I nodded and said, "Pleez excuse, little girl."

I walked to the phone, dialed, and waited for someone to pick up. I watched Jake trying to work up a lather of soap under the dripping softball.

"Kylie?" I said when she answered. "It's Heidi Elliott. Sign me up."

chapter/twelve

From: amorcita@springdale.net
To: anniebananie@wordlink.com
Subject: 34B?

Annie,
Need a new bra before you leave Roma for Greece? I
might be able to hook you up.
H

e ꙮ e

The second time I went to Kylie's house, I breezed right past
the Tabuchi without so much as a gawk. I was going to need to
get used to lifestyles of the rich and art-commissioning, I told
myself, raising my chin and doing my best runway model as
Kylie led me past the parlor, past a room she waved off as "the
ballroom," and past "one of the kitchens." My face expressed
no shock, no confusion when none of the pristine faucets in
the first kitchen were held together with duct tape. Get used
to it, sister, I told myself, already picturing my first spin in a
chocolate brown Mercedes.

After the first kitchen had segued into the catering kitchen, we reached the solarium. This appeared to be the north end of the house, finally. Three walls of glass let in rays of morning light. The room was expansive and bright, crowned with glass panes welded together with patinated copper. My intake of breath betrayed my lack of cool when I saw the view from the far wall. The solarium looked out onto the Zimmermans' backyard, which was roughly the size of Central Park but without the Rollerbladers, horse-drawn carriages, and poetic mourners in Strawberry Fields. The house stood on a hill, and acres of early summer green undulated across the grounds behind. To our right, five miles away, downtown Springdale nestled quietly, the horizon punctuated by church steeples and the college bell tower.

Kylie came to join me by the glass. "I'm so happy you called," she said, putting her arm around me as we watched a gardener spread mulch in a plot of miniature roses. "You're going to love working with Solomon's Closet."

I turned and smiled. "I think I will," I said. I took in an indulgence of white on the walls, the chair cushions, the couch. "This is such a pretty room. I can't believe how spotless it is with two children living in the same house."

"Oh, they aren't allowed in here," Kylie said, wrinkling her nose. "The children's wing is upstairs. They each have their own playroom, though Brenna's too young to use hers yet. The nanny knows she'd lose her job if they got into things on the main floor." She shook her head. "We've made far too great an investment to risk Popsicle stains."

"I see," I said, though I didn't at all. I had long ago given up the idea that my house was to be protected instead of lived in, which is probably why no one gasped with wonder when they visited *my* "solarium." "Does your nanny live with you?"

"Yes," Kylie said. She rubbed the back of her neck with her hand. "The girl up there right now is new. Anya, I think. We've had trouble keeping one around. It's a demanding job, taking care of two kids all day. Why do you think I hire it out?" She laughed loudly. "But then, I don't need to convince you of the hard work of parenting, do I?" She patted my arm.

"Definitely not."

"Well, SC is going to be a great outlet for you. You're going to wonder why you didn't start up the day Nora came home from the hospital."

I'd considered making voodoo doll pincushions out of my lingerie in the months after Nora's birth, so I didn't anticipate having any regrets about not selling lingerie sooner.

"This way," Kylie said, pointing toward an oval glass-topped table in the center of the room. I took a seat across from her and listened as we plowed through a brown and turquoise binder with a loopy SC on the front. We ran through basic sales techniques, how my income would be structured, and, my favorite part, the product line itself.

"Summer is a fantastic time to come on board," Kylie said. She opened a striped hat box and pulled out several bras, all size 32C, in light pastels. Each bra had a tag attached. I picked one up to read what was printed. "Pomegranate Garden Series," it said. "Song of Solomon 4:12-13."

"Each of our products is accompanied by a Scripture," Kylie said, seeing my confusion. "We are eager to remind ladies that their sensuality should not be something that embarrasses or shames them but that it is even celebrated in the Bible." She opened another hat box. "You know, Heidi," she said, pulling out a black nightie with a plunging neckline. The tag read "Faint with Love, Song of Solomon 5:8." "You will likely encounter people who simply will not understand what you do."

I thought of Laura Ingalls and her corduroy-jumper friend.

"But you know," Kylie continued, "we are fulfilling a need in the marketplace. It's an issue of supply and demand. Our numbers indicate that we're on to something and that women are eager to embrace their sensual selves. Even women of the church."

I was holding a bustier in a summery fruit print. The tag read "Comfort Me with Apples, Song of Solomon 2:5."

"I mean," Kylie said, really getting animated now, "we target a market ready and willing to spend money. The sales of religious books, gifts, and music have quadrupled in the last decade. We are a part of that movement. It's the perfect time to ride the wave."

I sat watching Kylie's flushed and eager face. I tried to ignore the bell of a cash register that seemed to accompany her words. She stopped suddenly, realizing I was staring. My hands were motionless on the Comforting Apples.

"And of course," she said, subdued, "we are happy to help all women, churched and otherwise, discover their fullest, most beautiful selves. Not only our clients, but especially our consultants." She smiled. "Like you."

I handed her a pile of garters to put back into the acccessories box. "Thanks," I said. "I hope this is a good fit."

"I have *no doubt* that it will be," she said. "Let me get you those postcards so you can set up your first party. Do you have a hostess in mind?"

I hadn't asked her yet, but I was pretty sure Willow would be game. "Yes," I said, taking a stack of invitations and catalogues from Kylie.

"We'll get you right into the swing of things," she said. "You'll have observed a couple of parties by then, so hosting your own will be a breeze." She cocked her head and smiled broadly. "How are you feeling about the beginning of your adventure?" she asked, leaning toward me like a middle school girlfriend across her desk.

"Great," I said. "I'm ready to give it a shot." I patted the stack of propaganda.

"You'll be a natural," Kylie said. She walked to a white desk in the corner of the room and clicked around a bit on a laptop. "And your total in start-up costs comes to . . . five hundred dollars. You can pay with check or credit card."

"Start-up costs?" I felt a heavy pit in my stomach. "I, uh, thought you said those would be waived."

"Did I?" Kylie said, her voice syrupy. Her brow furrowed in concern as she stared at the screen.

"The night of the party." I realized I was biting my nails and forced my hand down to my side.

"Oh, I see," Kylie said. "That offer was good for that evening only. You must have misunderstood."

"Right," I said. My heart was in my shoes. I tried not to picture Jake's face when I relayed this tidbit of information. "You said you'd take credit card?"

Kylie ran my MasterCard through her machine and said, "I know this must feel like a lot of money, Heidi, but I assure you it is a very small investment compared with what you'll gain. There isn't a stock on the market that can offer what

Solomon's Closet does in terms of monetary return."

I nodded mutely. She had to be right, I thought, looking around at *la casa de los* Zimmerman. You couldn't get to 11 Ridgecrest without sound investments, right?

Kylie handed me my receipt and helped me gather my things. I followed her out of the solarium and back to the front entrance.

"Call me anytime, Heidi," she said. "I'm always willing to hear your questions and concerns. Your success is my success." She opened the front double doors to the noonday sun. She lifted her face. "Mmm," she said. "I'm tempted to ask Maria or Sasha or whatever her name is to work a double shift on a day like today."

"Ah, yes," I agreed, picturing my own in-house nanny, Jake, in one of those black French maid numbers with white eyelet trim, holding a feather duster. I bit back a giggle.

"Enjoy the sunshine," Kylie said, waving at me as I descended the steps onto the circular driveway. I waved as she shut the door, waiting until she was out of sight to check under the Beast for any oil spots. I breathed a sigh of relief when I saw that the bricks were clear of my car's droppings. Not good to be the one dirtying the missus's property.

I revved the engine on my way down the hill, head spinning with rose gardens, glass walls, a credit card receipt, and my new career.

℮ ℈ ℮

To my delight, the five hundred dollar investment discussion resolved much more peacefully than anticipated. After the initial ashen face and gulp of water, Jake allowed himself to be persuaded by his wife, saleswoman-in-training.

"After all, Warren Buffett always says," I instructed, "you've got to spend money to make money."

"That right?" Jake said, one eyebrow arched. "Warren would know."

"Exactly," I said, clapping my hands for emphasis. "Warren would certainly know."

"Then again," Jake said, his arms behind his head, "Warren can't possibly spend all his money in the years he has left on this earth, so he can be more flippant than we Elliotts."

"Are you okay with this?" I asked, sitting on his lap. Dinner was over, dishes cleared. Nora was in bed early, tuckered out after a day of sunshine and fiercely draining fingerpainting.

"Yes," Jake said. He kissed me on the lips. "You're going to be really good at selling skanky lingerie to unsuspecting church women. It's right up your alley."

"Not the compliment I'd envisioned, but at least you're not mad about the money."

"I can't be mad. I'm off to play Ultimate." Jake and Rob, a buddy from work, were members of a citywide Ultimate Frisbee league. Like golf, Ultimate was a great excuse to play outdoors. Unlike golf, however, the only cost involved was the price of a Frisbee. Plus, there were health benefits to running the length of a soccer field nonstop for two hours. I could not grasp these benefits myself, but I lauded anyone who could.

"Have fun," I said, slapping his rear as a benediction. "I'll expect that to be tighter upon your return."

"Impossible," Jake said, grinning as he jogged down the driveway and toward our neighborhood park.

I sat down on the porch swing to read. To be honest, my book served merely as an excuse to sit and watch my neighbors across the street. I was the type of girl who hoped for long delays in airports because of the people-watching opportunities. Give me a seat in a ballpark, subway station, or interstate rest stop, and I was good to go for hours. Once, on a trip to New York, Jake had to bribe me with chocolate to get me to leave a bench I'd procured on some artsy corner in Brooklyn. But I was equally happy in the food court at Springdale's Westridge Mall. I didn't need purple hair or nipple rings to find my fellow humans interesting. People eating their cheese curds sufficed.

Given my simple needs, then, I would have been content to have any elderly couple living across the street from me. But God loved me and must have wanted me to not only enjoy sitting on the porch but to look for times I could send my husband to play Frisbee just so I could watch the Angelos.

Martin and Louise Angelo were in their early seventies and were better viewing than *Real World* reruns. Martin was a retired engineer-turned-entrepreneur, perpetually on the porch tinkering with incongruous pairings like telephone wire and a flamethrower, or an empty milk carton and a fishing pole. He'd lean over the invention at hand, brow furrowed and lips pursed, occasionally muttering to himself or swearing at the announcer on talk radio. Martin was short with a shock of thick white hair slicked back with what Jake called "product" and Martin probably called "grease." At various times, I'd suspected Martin to be Native American (when he went through a headdress phase), Latino (when he'd hung a Mexican flag on Cinco de Mayo), and even part Chinese (when I caught him doing tai chi on his lawn one morning). But then he'd brought over a mason jar of green beer on St. Paddy's Day and told us about his Irish grandmother. I must have looked confused because he'd laughed and said he liked to think of himself as "ethnically flexible."

So Martin was enough entertainment on his own but with Louise, he turned in Academy Award–winning performances on a regular basis. Louise was a slip of a thing, no more than ninety pounds and barely over five feet. She usually had her hair in rollers but around the pink foam peeked strawberry blonde out of a bottle. Louise preferred a particular uniform, which she wore indoors and outdoors during all four seasons and varied only in color and accessories. That day, I watched her scurry out of her front door in one of her knee-length silk robes, this one sapphire blue and printed with Chinese characters, orchids, and birds of paradise. Her face was heavily made up, the coral lipstick layered generously around her mouth a lovely complement to sky blue eye shadow.

"Martin," she said, hurrying toward her husband like a hissing goose. Even Louise's whispers were stage whispers, as both she and Martin were hard of hearing.

Martin didn't look up from his Bunsen burner. "Mmm?"

"That was your sister on the phone. She wants to visit. *Again.*"

"Mmm," Martin said and then cursed when he burned his finger. "Louise," he said, "this is not a good time."

"It most certainly is, Mister Man," Louise said, reaching over to extinguish the little flame. "I've been married to you for fifty-one years, Martin Angelo, and I will not play second fiddle to a Bunsen burner."

Martin turned to face her. He pulled off his protective eyewear and tossed the rubber glasses onto the driveway. "Well, the learning curve must be pretty long around here, then, because after all those years you should have figured out not to bother me when I'm working."

Louise let out a high-pitched cackle. "Working? You think this is working? Maybe I should join you and bring out my *knitting*. Then we could both *work* together."

"You don't knit, you crazy woman," Martin seethed. "Though maybe that would be a good thing to take up. Domesticate you a little bit."

"Wouldn't that just float your boat," Louise said, both hands on her little hips. "Then you could have that boring life you've always wanted. When I'm dead and gone, I'm sure your second wife will be happy to have your sister visit anytime. In fact, maybe she'll come *live* with you so you can all be cranky old domestic dimwits together."

"Is that what you think?" Martin asked, taking the burner and tossing it into the bushes. He met Louise's fiery gaze, took her by her diminutive shoulders, and kissed her.

She pulled her face away, gasping and trying not to laugh. "Dirty old man," she said and wiggled to escape his grasp.

"You have no idea, woman," Martin said, pulling her closer. I worried that silk sash tying it all together wouldn't be able to withstand this much roughhousing.

Louise giggled and shook her head. She patted her curlers, her fingers sprinkled with sunspots and wrinkles but her nails perfectly painted the color of her lipstick. "My father was right about you." She slipped out of Martin's embrace and scampered for their front door.

"He sure was," Martin said, following her into the house.

I made a mental note to include Louise in my Solomon's Closet clientele.

And this was typical, I'm telling you. I hadn't watched much during the winter because I was a ninny about the cold, but Martin and Louise had been out there, one of them more appropriately clothed than the other. Today's argument had a quick resolution, but they had been known to box it out for days, taking breaks only to eat ramen noodles in their small kitchen, visible from my side of the street. I had given up cable entirely since discovering the Angelos.

Show over, I went inside and made a cup of mango tea before sitting down at the computer. I sipped as I booted up, letting the tea warm and relax me for the night's sleep. My plan was to do a quick e-mail check before getting in bed with a good book. I thought I'd relay the Angelo sighting to Annie, give her a hint of all the excitement she was missing in small-town America.

My in-box showed a new message from her. I clicked.

From: anniebananie@wordlink.com
To: amorcita@springdale.net
Subject: Amore

Heidi,

I really wish I could call to tell you all this but it's some crazy hour in Springdale and I can't wait until tomorrow. So forgive me for telling you about the most important day of my life through an e-mail.

I think I'm in love.

His name is James and don't worry: he's not Italian and won't be stealing me from America and you. He's actually from Boston but here in Milan on business. (BTW, did I tell you I'm in Milan now? I postponed Greece because I just didn't feel done with Italy and now ... well, I'll get to that.) I met him in the piazza outside La Scala (famous opera house, Verdi, yada yada). I was eating gelato by the statue of DaVinci (Can you believe this? It's so Audrey Hepburn!), and he asked if I was American. I tried feeling insulted. It wasn't like I was wearing a fanny pack. But I couldn't get past this man's face.

Heidi, I'm telling you. Gorgeous. Like in a famous actor sort of way. Think suave like George Clooney, delicious like Denzel, and the swagger of Reese Witherspoon's ex in *Sweet Home . . .* I'm serious. All in one man.

So we talked by the fountain, then on a walk around Milan, then over drinks, which turned into dinner, which turned into drinks again, then dancing ... You get the picture. I just got back to my room and I've counted. I spent twelve straight hours with this man.

Don't puke but I already miss him.

So I'm trying not to be but I think I'm in love.

Did I mention James is African American? It occurs to me as I picture you reading this in good old lily-white Springdale that this might be a point of interest. To be honest, it has nothing to do with today, so I almost forgot to tell you.

I'm starting to crash — so sleepy. James is in Milan for two more weeks, so I'll be here. Will write again soon.

Love you, Heids. Aren't you happy for me? Beats the heck out of redoing my kitchen tile. . . .

Annie

Wow.

I sat staring at Annie's letter for minutes, forgetting to blink until my eyes started to tear. Annie's in love, I thought, trying to wrap my head around what that might look like. Annie had certainly loved men before. Her relationship with Ben was loving, I'd say. But this Annie sounded breathless and girlish, not a whole lot like the Annie who cleaned teeth and organized her sock drawer for fun.

James. I didn't even know a last name.

I'm really happy for her, I told myself, signing off and shutting down the computer so I could sleep on a reply. Annie deserved to feel heart-stopping love, even if it was in a foreign country with a man I hadn't screened.

I was happy for her.

I dumped the remnants of my tea into the kitchen sink and walked to my bedroom. After trudging through two chapters of a novel, I gave up and shut the book. Staring straight ahead, I listened to the silence of my house.

God, I prayed, You love Annie even more than I do, which is insane. I've prayed it before and I'll pray it again: Please draw her to You. Maybe even through this James character.

I sighed, feeling that tug that Willow calls the Spirit and that I think is the pushiest silence known to humans.

As long as You're in the groove, I added, would you draw me to You, too? The irony of this whole thing is that the more I know You, the more I need You.

I must have fallen asleep because the next thing I remember is Jake slipping under the comforter with me.

"Annie's in love with a man named James," I mumbled. "He's perfect and black and from Boston."

"Our Annie's in love?" Jake asked, draping an arm and a leg around me.

"His name is James," I said before drifting back into my dream about George Clooney and Denzel Washington stopping by for ice cream and Bunsen burner s'mores.

chapter/thirteen

"Just tell me," I said. It was a steamy morning in July. Nora was still asleep, the only noise on the monitor the low hum of her box fan. I sat very still on the edge of the bed, talking to Jake, who stood with his back to me in the doorway of the master bathroom. I could see a sliver of his face in the reflection of the mirror.

He turned to me with a somber face. "Negative."

I averted my gaze. "Thought so." I bit my lip and tried not to cry.

Jake sat down next to me and pulled me to him. "But we're not upset, right? Because we haven't been trying very long, right?"

"Three months," I said into his T-shirt.

"Right. Three months. And they say it takes six months to a year to conceive, right?"

I said nothing.

"So that would still put us at the 'Oh my gosh, I can't believe I'm already pregnant' stage were we to conceive anytime in the next three months, right?"

I lifted my face and looked at Jake. "I think there's something wrong."

"Heidi."

"I'm serious." I brushed away a hot tear. "We got pregnant with Nora right away. I don't even know if I'm ovulating."

Jake sighed. "I thought we'd agreed that we weren't going to get stressed out about this. That we'd just relax and let God take care of the timing."

"But God doesn't tell us to ignore our intuition that something is probably, definitely wrong."

"Heids," Jake said, taking both my hands in his. "I really don't think there is anything wrong with you. Or me. Or my boys." His mouth crept into a smile.

"This is not about your virility, Jake," I said, my voice rising a whole step in pitch. "I just think we should make sure everything is okay. What if there's something wrong and we can fix it? What if there's something we should be doing now? Why would we waste a year of trying just because we want to pretend we're relaxed?" I was squeezing his hands.

He pried my fingernails out of his skin. "I wasn't exactly pretending," he said, wincing. He looked at me, long and unblinking. "So what are you suggesting? We go to a doctor?"

"Just me," I said. "I'll make an appointment with my OB to check out the equipment and make sure everything is on the up-and-up."

Jake shook his head. "I don't even want to know how that's done." He leaned over to kiss my lips. "But we're still praying about this, right? God's still in our inner circle?"

"Absolutely," I said and kissed him again. "We're just utilizing the gift of modern medicine."

Jake let himself fall back on the bed. "They're not going to want to watch the boys under a microscope, are they?"

bottom line   147

"Good grief," I said, pouncing on him. "I wish you thought of me as often as you think of your boys. Let's wrestle." I pinned one of his shoulders with my elbow. I'm fierce in the ring.

He flipped me over and said, "Thoughts of you and my boys are directly related."

"Sick," I said, slipping out from under him and positioning myself for my other fail-safe play, a headlock. I moved fast, knowing that my ultimate resort, tickling the ribs, was only one move away.

℮ ⅾ ℮

I arrived at Maybelle's house fifteen minutes before the party was to start. This was my chance to see Kylie work her magic at a "home-hosted Solomon's Closet experience." Maybelle Walker had agreed to open her home to eight of her friends in exchange for deep discounts on the summer line.

"Maybelle, meet Heidi," Kylie said when they greeted me on the front step of a midsized brick ranch on the east side of town. "Heidi is a new member of the SC team and will be observing today."

"Good to meet you," Maybelle said in a husky voice, grasping my hand. She looked to be about sixty, though she carried herself as a woman half her age. Plump and saucy, this one. I winced under the pressure of large jeweled rings circling each of Maybelle's fingers. "Please come in," she said, propping the screen door open with her arm.

I thanked her and stepped into a dimly lit living room.

Maybelle gestured with her hand as if inviting me into the Ritz. "Welcome to our little piece of paradise."

A generous interpretation, it turned out. Against Maybelle's better judgment, the room was decorated in a cowboy motif. Wrought iron was everywhere: woven into a remarkable dried flower arrangement on the wall above an upright piano, shaped into lassoes and cowboy hats on a wicker bookshelf, and accenting a large portrait of Maybelle and a man I assumed was her husband.

"You have a lovely home," I lied, smiling brightly at our hostess.

Kylie cleared her throat. "Bud worked on a Montana ranch years ago, didn't he, Maybelle?"

Maybelle chuckled, her voice around the timbre of James Earl Jones'. "I'll tell you what, girls," she said, slowly shaking platinum blonde curls piled high on her head. "Can't take the Montana out of a boy, if you know what I'm saying."

Judging by the vacant smile on Kylie's face, I don't believe she did.

The doorbell rang and Maybelle scooted off to welcome her first arrival, a hunched woman from next door named Fran. Fran's hair was white with a bluish hue. She smiled at Maybelle, and her face dissolved into a million wrinkles. In that moment, I hoped for the same effect when I was Fran's age, a sort of epidermal trophy earned after years of smiling. Maybelle gave Fran a gentle hug to avoid breaking any fragile bones.

"Thank God I came early to light the candles," Kylie muttered to me after Maybelle had left to serve Fran a cup of pink punch, heavy on the sherbet. "With all the windows open and five candles lit, we're almost to the point where we won't asphyxiate from secondhand smoke." Kylie wasn't doing a very good job of masking her disgust, though I suppose it didn't matter as long as I was the only one within earshot. "And the food she's serving," Kylie said and shuddered.

I peeked around Kylie for a look at the table. I could see a tray of deviled eggs, some store-bought wafer cookies, and a glass dish of pickles, carrots, and dip. Maybelle had strewn fake rose petals over the light pink tablecloth.

Kylie pursed her lips. "We encourage our hostesses to keep refreshments to a minimum, if they serve anything at all. Coffee or tea, maybe a simple dessert. That way the focus remains on the products, there's less risk of spills and stains, et cetera." She shot a glance at Maybelle's frothing punch bowl and sighed. "But what can you do? I've just had to accept that some things lie outside my realm of control. I cannot teach a person *class*." She was staring at a pile of plastic trays stacked up by the plate of wafers.

"Kylie," Maybelle called from across the room.

In a nanosecond, Kylie's face changed to reflect nothing but joy, warmth, and a deep love for cowboy decor and packaged cookies. "Maybelle, how can I help you?" she asked, moving toward the hostess and patting Fran's hand on the way. Fran smiled, looking pleased with Kylie's graciousness.

Ten minutes later, all the guests had arrived. Maybelle's posse was a mix of neighbors and friends from her church, First Pentecostal on Fuller Road. Fran turned out to be the oldest in the group. Most of the women were middle-aged, though one had brought her daughter, a sullen woman in her early twenties. The daughter, Candy, looked to be about nine and a half months pregnant and angry to be humoring any sort of discussion of sex.

"Ladies, welcome," Kylie said after we were settled in chairs around Maybelle's living room. I'd considered sitting on the saddle displayed next to a mammoth fern, but had deferred. Something told me that wouldn't have gone over so well with Boss Kylie.

"Thank you all for coming today to enjoy a few hours away from your busy lives to relax and hang out with the girls." Kylie's smile was conspiratorial, and the room twittered with approval. Even Fran looked pleased to have escaped for some girl time.

I watched for the next hour as Kylie worked that crowd like Wayne Newton. She was warm, she was attentive, and she made those women feel like queens.

"Now," she said when things were still warming up, "at Solomon's Closet, our goal is to give women tools to *reclaim* how beautiful and unique they truly are. Not by comparing them to a skinny runway model who eats saltine crackers to survive."

The ladies laughed and nodded appreciatively.

"Not by pressuring you to buy a product or spend money on purchases you'll regret later." Kylie said this as if having these women fork over cash was downright distasteful to her. "But so women like you, women like me, can feel gorgeous, wanted, and, yes, sexy in our own skin and in our own bedroom. And all this for the glory of the God who created women and created sex."

The Pentecostals weren't afraid to "amen," and they did so with exuberance. I wondered if Kylie changed her delivery according to denomination. I couldn't see Episcopalians getting as riled up about sex for the glory of God.

Kylie worked her way through the summer line, masterfully tailoring her spiel to emphasize what she thought would trip the triggers of the ladies at Maybelle's house. Maybelle, for example, was concerned about support for her ample bosom, complaining that most of the bras she'd owned in her adult life had either been too small and had straps that dug into her shoulders or looked like something her mother would wear. "Bud finally just asked me to take that nasty harness off before it could ruin the mood," she said, her laughter interrupted by a raucous coughing fit.

Kylie was ready with a sample from our Real Women line before Maybelle had finished hacking. My boss seemed to have a genius knack for anticipating the sale, no matter the woman, no matter the figure. Even Candy bought three teddies with pretty folds of fabric gathered around the middle, anticipating postpartum moments when her husband would be ready to resume but her body would still need a little propping and prodding.

"Just what I should *not* be doing," Candy said, shaking her head but smiling as she wrote a check.

We had bidden farewell to the last guest and were helping Maybelle tidy up when Bud came home. He slammed the front door and walked inside. Moseyed, rather.

"Hello there, ladies," Bud said, taking off a real-life cowboy hat and hanging it on the coatrack. "Bud Walker." A weathered and tanned face looked down at us and smiled.

I accepted his hand. "Heidi Elliott. Nice to meet you, Bud."

Kylie shook Bud's hand as well, nodding and sizing up his bolero tie and worn Levis. "You have a lovely home and an even lovelier wife, Bud."

"Don't I know it," Bud said, ambling over to Maybelle and giving her a quick slap on the rear.

"Bud, for goodness' sake," Maybelle said, trying to look appalled.

Bud took Maybelle's jeweled hand and spun her around and into a low dip. "This woman chose me out of the whole bunch. Ain't I one lucky man?" He planted a kiss on Maybelle's lips.

Kylie and I were watching, she with a faint tinge of horror and I with a slaphappy grin. Wrought iron and lassoes or not, I was a sucker for love.

"Yes, well, I believe you are," Kylie said, her smile unmoving. "We'll get out of your way then." She hefted her party supplies and made for the door.

I wasn't quite ready. "How long have you two been married?" I asked.

"Oh, what is it now, baby?" Bud said, looking at Maybelle. "Thirty-seven? No, thirty-eight. Thirty-eight years this April."

I nodded appreciatively. "Congratulations. You make a great couple."

"Well, thank you, honey," Maybelle said, letting Bud hug her around the middle. "It hasn't always been easy, but the making up has always been good."

Bud chuckled. "You girls might not have noticed yet, but this one's a real firecracker." He looked at Maybelle. "Did you tell 'em about the time you threw your wedding ring out the car window into a cornfield? While I was going sixty-five down the 110?"

Maybelle pursed her lips. "Hush, you old fool. You think we talked about things like that at a classy ladies' get-together? This was a well-behaved affair."

Bud snorted. "Wasn't this the bra and panty party?"

"Solomon's Closet," Kylie interjected, one foot already on the front step. "Fine lingerie for the woman of faith. I'll be in touch, Maybelle," she said and waved as she scurried down the walk.

"Good to meet you two," I said. "Bud, you behave yourself when that order comes in."

Bud laughed, slapped his knee. "Now what fun is that?"

I waved. The Walkers let the door close behind me. I thought I heard Maybelle squealing.

Kylie motioned me over to the back of her Mercedes SUV, where she was loading her party supplies. "You don't have to do that, you know," she said quietly.

"Do what?"

"Talk like that. Chitchat, compliment them on their marriage. Endure that mindless chatter."

I looked at her like she was missing a few. "That wasn't charity," I said, my heart rate starting to pick up speed. "Bud and Maybelle seem great. I enjoyed talking with them."

Kylie rolled her eyes. "Whatever. Just know that once the party's over, you're free to go as soon as you can. People don't need us to hang around."

I stood straighter. "I don't think we were bothering them. Plus, didn't you get a kick out of Bud's antics? And how much they like each other after all these years?"

Kylie sniffed. "Not really. I've seen it all in this business. Two weeks from now they could be divorced and fighting about who gets the saddle." She shook her head, disdain all over her face. "You never know what goes on behind closed doors."

Actually, I thought I had a pretty good idea what was going on behind the Walkers' closed doors, but I kept it to myself.

"Anyway," Kylie said, slamming shut her back hatch, "I thought the day went well. I'll run the numbers at home and give you an exact total, but I'm thinking the gross is somewhere around fifteen hundred."

I gulped. "Dollars? In an hour and a half?"

She nodded. "Which means I net about seven fifty. You won't start out with that high a percentage, but you'll get there."

Seven hundred fifty dollars. I could hear Jake clicking his heels from here.

"I'll call you, Heidi." Kylie started her engine, reaching quickly to turn down her stereo. "Eye of the Tiger" had been playing at full volume. She looked at me sheepishly and shrugged. "Helps me get ready for a sale."

I nodded and bit my cheek.

"See you soon," Kylie said. She pulled away from the curb and waved in the rearview mirror as she sped away.

When she was out of sight, I did a few shadow punches à la Rocky Balboa, just to get it out of my system. Then I climbed into my Civic, buckled up, and grooved to Al Green all the way home.

ℰ ℈ ℰ

I was teaching first period to a full classroom at Springdale High. The class was clearly not taking me seriously because I was buck naked. I'd tried everything to get them to focus on the subjunctive tense and was ready to resort to interpretive dance when I woke up, shaking. A dream, I told myself, hearing Jake's loud breathing and the telephone ringing.

I squinted at the digital clock on my bedside table: 5:06 a.m. Who in their right mind would be calling at such an hour? If this yokel wakes up Nora, I thought, stumbling out of bed and toward the phone in the kitchen. "Hello?" I said, barely audible around sleepy vocal chords. Nothing. I tried again, this time too loudly in our silent house. "Hello?"

"Heidi! It's me!"

"Annie. My good gracious. Are you all right?"

She giggled. "I am *so* all right. Are you all right?"

I sighed. "Annie, are you drunk? You sound drunk."

"Absolutely not, and I'm offended you would ask."

I rubbed my eyes. "It's five o'clock in the morning."

"I'm so sorry, Heids. I know it's early for you but I needed to talk with you and couldn't wait another hour."

"Are you still in Milan?" I said through a yawn. "It's good to hear your voice, even if it is in total darkness and through the haze of REM."

"Remember R.E.M.? Whatever happened to them?"

"Annie?"

"What? Oh. Right. Why I'm calling at this hour. Heidi Elliott, I'm going to need a maid of honor. Or matron, I guess, in your case."

My puffy eyes were wide open. "You're kidding."

"I'm not!" she squealed. "In fact, I've never been so seriously happy in my life. Heidi, you are not going to believe this man. He is *perfect*."

Completely false, but a symptom of her illness. "Wow. Annie. I can't believe it." My head was reeling. "I mean, congratulations."

"Thank you," she said, her voice melodious. "I can't wait for you two to meet. You're going to love him."

"I'm sure I will." Jake had appeared in the kitchen, hair standing at attention and a confused look on his face. "Annie's engaged," I whispered with my hand over the mouthpiece.

Jake's puffy lids got imperceptibly wider. "To Jason?"

"James," I corrected. "Go back to bed."

Jake nodded and shuffled off.

". . . when we get back at Thanksgiving?" Annie was saying when I tuned back in.

"What about Thanksgiving?"

"That's when you can meet James. He'll be back in the States before then for a while, but then he'll meet up with me here for a couple of weeks and we'll fly home to Springdale. Heidi, I'm finally understanding what it feels like to *fit* with someone. Like you and Jake. It's amazing, isn't it?"

All right. This needed to end before she started singing or something. "It really is. Give James our congrats and e-mail me all the gory details as soon as you can, okay? Love you, Annie."

"I love you, too, Heidi. And love is a many-splendored thing, you know."

"Right. Bye, Annie."

"Ciao, amica bella."

I clicked to hang up and sat on the kitchen floor, knees pulled to my chest. She's engaged, I thought. I haven't even met him, much less decided he's worthy of her. He could be a mass murderer, for crying out loud. I bit my thumbnail. How does she know he's not part of some scam? Hadn't we seen that Leo DiCaprio film together? That one about the man with a zillion different identities who conned innocent people into giving him their life's riches? Or maybe that was the one with Jennifer Love Hewitt and Sigourney Weaver. . . . At any rate, these people did exist in the world.

She probably hasn't even Googled him, I thought disgruntledly as I hefted myself from the floor and headed back to bed. I crawled in beside Jake and formed my body to his.

"She's getting married," I whispered.

"Hmm," Jake said, not quite as floored by the news.

"What if he's a creep? What if he's one of those people from *Montel* who has a different set of wife and kids in every city?" I listened to Jake inhale, exhale. "*Sure*, his name is James. *Sure*, he's from Boston. For all we know, his name is Spike and he lives in his mother's basement under fluorescent lights with a Maltese named Precious."

"Heidi," Jake said in a very awake voice.

"I thought you were sleeping."

"That is my goal, yes."

"You want to talk about this later?"

"Please."

"Okay," I said, sighing. "Good night."

Jake *hmphed* and snuggled his head into his pillow.

"I mean, 'Good morning.'"

I thought I heard a quiet groan. I rolled to my back and watched the light creep in until the room was washed in the pale yellow of a July dawn.

chapter/fourteen

"Item 47568b, The Delilah, Lavender," I muttered, sifting through the pile of lingerie on my lap. "Delilah, Delilah . . . here." I tossed the teddy into one of the turquoise and brown hat boxes that formed a semicircle around me.

"I *love* this bracelet," cooed Nora, lifting a pink and white polka-dot garter belt out of one of the boxes.

"Norie, honey," I said, trying to keep frustration from elevating my volume or pitch. "I know these look like fun things to touch, but please keep them in the boxes. You can be here, but you have to keep your hands off Mommy's things. How about you draw a picture for Daddy that he can take to work on Monday?" I went back to my muttering. "87953a. Gaza Strip Tease Fun Pack."

Three items later, I saw Jake approach out of the corner of my eye. He shifted on his feet as he stood above me. "Um, Heidi?" he said.

I looked up at him and then followed his gaze to our daughter.

"I'm pretty!" Nora announced triumphantly, her eyelashes fluttering behind pink-tinted Dora the Explorer glasses. Over her blue gingham sundress, she'd pulled her legs into a lacy, racy yellow thong.

Nora twirled to give us the full picture. "Yellow is my *favorite*."

Jake looked at me, one eyebrow raised. "That stuff gets by the Christians, huh?"

I shot him a fiery glance. "What? Christians can't wear thongs?"

"Shh," Jake said, nodding toward the exhibitionist in the room. "Miss Steel Trap will definitely make inopportune use of that word."

"Well, you can't have it both ways, Jake," I said, getting back to my inventory. "You want me to make some cash and you like having sex with your Christian wife. And yet you don't think other Christians should be having sex or talking about it or making money from it?"

"Whoa there, Spice Girl," Jake said, hands up in defense. "I never said any of those things. I never even said you needed to get a job. And I certainly think Christians should have great sex. Last night, for example—"

"Shh," I said. "Steel trap."

"Anyway," Jake said with a slow grin. "If my wife has to be selling something, I can't think of anything I'd like better than boxes full of booty wear."

"Lingerie," I corrected, rolling my eyes. "And now you see why men are never invited to a Solomon's Closet event." I picked up Nora's thong, now discarded, and hid it in a box behind my back.

"Blatant discrimination." Jake grabbed the papers out of my hand and set them down on the floor. He pulled me to my feet. "I'm filing a suit."

"Sure you are," I said, letting him lead me in a musicless

waltz. Just as good, considering our familial lack of rhythm. "You'd be the first husband to complain of the aftereffects of Solomon's Closet on his wife and marriage."

"You have a point," Jake said, hand above my head to give me a spin.

I twirled back into him and stopped, looking up. "I'm a little nervous."

"About the party?" he asked.

I nodded. My first party was scheduled for that afternoon at Willow's house. Depending on the moment, I felt excited, nervous, and/or fearful that I'd sell not even one bottle of Gilead Body Glitter.

"You're going to be awesome," Jake said. He dropped me into a low dip, my head inches from the floor.

Nora noticed and clapped. "My turn, Daddy." She tossed her crayon onto the unfinished drawing.

"You really think so?" I asked. I felt queasy, my thoughts on the miserable experience of selling Kit Kats door-to-door for middle school band.

Jake pulled me upward from my prone position.

"Daddy, Daddy, it's my turn." Nora was jumping up and down between us. "Can I try, please, please?"

"Sure, peanut," Jake said. He lifted Nora in his arms. They began their dance and Jake looked at me. "I'm sorry—what did you ask?"

"Nothing," I said, dropping to the floor again to finish my work. "I just don't know if I'm cut out for this sort of thing."

"You'll be great, Heids," Jake said. Nora giggled as he spun her around the family room, arms outstretched for a cheek-to-cheek tango. "Nora, tell your mother she'll be great."

"You're great, Mommy," Nora said, gasping for air amid fits of giggles.

I watched them a moment. Upon her insistence, Jake plunged Nora into five dips in a row. When her complexion started showing shades of green, he stopped, though even then she protested.

This is not middle school band sales, I reminded myself as I dug into a pile of plus-sized panties. I might have called Kylie for a pep talk but decided she was not a person who felt comfortable around self-doubt.

Minutes later, her green face pink once more, Nora convinced Jake to attempt another round of dips. I finished counting, listing, and sorting and hoped that in the Elliott family, Nora was the only glutton for punishment.

☙ ❧ ☙

"You look great," Willow said, hugging me as I entered her home.

"Thanks," I said and exhaled loudly. "I'm nervous."

"Don't be," she said, taking turquoise and brown striped hat boxes from me and setting them down on the entryway bench. "You'll be a natural. Plus, it will be fun to see everyone again."

Willow had invited a slew of women she knew, most of them from our on-hiatus Moms' Group at First Lutheran. In the absence of Molly's fearless leadership, all the girls hadn't gotten together in months. When I was able to distract myself from the butterfly colony in my stomach, I felt excited to see our motley crew reunited.

I stood on the threshold of the living room, taking in the comfort of Willow's home. During the last three years, Willow had held her doors open to me, Jake, and Nora. This house had been a harbor, on days when I'd searched the Internet for circus openings and on days when my life felt like a pair of tailor-made jeans.

Willow led me down the center hallway, our feet making creaky music with the well-worn floor. We arrived in the kitchen. Willow walked over to the stove and I sat at the kitchen table.

"I love this house," I said, smiling at the stacks of bright Fiestaware showing off in the glass-front cupboards.

Willow poured boiling water from a copper teapot. She handed me a steaming cup, the smell of fresh mint permeating the room. "I love it, too."

We sat at a circular table Willow had purchased in an estate sale when she and Michael were newly married. The warm oak had been the scene of countless meals, first with just the two of them, then as their family grew to include their three sons, and now just Willow and her sixteen-year-old twins, Stream and Blue. Her oldest, Hike, was off at college.

Willow's bright green eyes were a match for the color of the walls. "This room in particular has seen a lot of action through the years," she said, her eyes crinkling with memory.

"And probably enough food to feed sub-Saharan Africa."

Willow laughed. "Exactly. Three teenage boys would have made anyone panic, but Michael was actually the worst. He was tall and thin, but the man could eat an alarming amount of food."

Until the end, I thought, wondering if Willow was

thinking the same. How long does it take for the jagged edges of difficult memories to wear down? When do they become soft enough to hold without cutting one's hands to bits?

"Come," Willow said, pushing back her chair. "We only have a few minutes before party time and I want you to see the spread."

I followed her into the living room. The walls, which had changed color three times in three years, were currently chocolate brown. Willow had amassed quite the art collection through her work with the gallery. Some selections on the walls changed as often as the paint color, though it was always with joy that I viewed a few of her perennial favorites: a small original watercolor by O'Keeffe and a series of etchings by a local artist. These, in particular, looked beautiful against the brown wall.

"Love the current exhibit, Madame Gallery Owner."

"Don't make fun. You know I like things to change every now and then."

"I'm not making fun. I never make fun of people who feed me. Everything looks perfect."

She smiled as we looked at the goodies she'd set up on a side table against the wall. Croissants paired with raspberry, cherry, and apricot preserves, a braided sweet bread topped with toasted almonds, an oblong silver dish filled with fruit, and a platter piled with decadent-looking chocolate cookies.

"Lupe is amazing," Willow said. "She made everything but the cookies."

"Lupe deserves a raise," I said, picking up a croissant to nibble. Lupe was a striking young woman with night black hair and coffee eyes who had recently emigrated from Colombia to

Springdale. She'd trained at the culinary school in Bogotá. Soon after her move to Minnesota, she'd brought Willow a basket of goodies at the art gallery. One bite into her raspberry *tartaleta* and Lupe landed herself a job as pastry chef for The Loft.

"Just got one," Willow said, taking a toothpick to spear a slice of kiwi. "She's growing our business like mad. She deserves it." She tipped her head toward the plate of cookies. "Try one of those."

"I will later. But if they aren't Lupe creations, who made them?"

Willow was silent long enough for me to turn and look at her face. She was blushing, always a Kodachrome event with a redhead.

"We made them."

"The boys helped you? Very sweet. Why are you bright red? Quality time embarrasses you?"

She bit her bottom lip. "The boys weren't exactly home. I meant I made them with, um, a man I've been seeing."

"What?!" I know shrieking should be reserved for things like pterodactyls and cockatoos, but I couldn't contain myself. "You're dating someone? What's his name? Do I know him?"

Willow allowed herself a small smile. "His name is David and—"

The doorbell rang.

"Ignore that," I said, my hands on Willow's shoulders to turn her toward the kitchen. "Those people don't need any of what I'm selling anyway. Let's talk about David."

Willow scooted away from my herding. "Heidi," she said, laughing. "I'm getting the door. We'll talk about my love life later."

"Wait," I said, hurrying around to block her path to the door. "I'm not ready."

"Yes, you are," Willow said, gently manhandling me to get out of her way. "You need to just do this. In two hours it will all be over."

She swished past me in her floor-length batik skirt and I was left alone, wishing I could hide under her Bolivian woven tablecloth.

"Well, look who's gonna make some money off me today." Neesha Jackson entered the room and headed toward me with open arms.

"Neesha, thanks for coming," I said, letting her crush me with a hug. Her braids smelled of honey and coconut. "How are you?"

She shook her head. "Girl, don't ask. Jeremy has the kids today but it doesn't even count with all his *moaning* about it." She shook her head. I always felt I should kneel or something in Neesha's presence. She was a dead ringer for African royalty.

It was good to see everyone again. Molly was there, still a front-runner in the campaign to bring back eighties fashion. That afternoon, for example, she wore an orange and magenta skort with matching headband, nearly lost behind a healthy crop of Aqua Net bangs. The effect was chilling.

"Heidi, I've *so* missed you," Molly said. When it came to petite and sassy Molly Langdon, one should not confuse size with force of impact.

"It's great to see you, Molly," I said. "Thank you for coming."

"Would not *miss it*," she said, shrugging her shoulder pads before moving over to the croissants.

Most of the guests had arrived. I spotted several other familiar faces. Shelly was a plus-sized pack of dynamite and would likely have a running commentary about Solomon's Closet. She would balance out Faith, a quiet woman with black hair that hung in a shiny blanket to her shoulders. She smiled and waved from across the room, dark brown almond-shaped eyes framed by cat-eye glasses.

I ducked into the tiny bathroom off the kitchen and shut the door quietly behind me. I stood in front of the mirror, wishing I'd listened to Kylie's motivational CDs. I shook my head at my bad self. "What are you doing, you freak?" I whispered to my reflection.

"I'll tell you what you're doing," I answered, trying my best to sound like Kylie at Maybelle's house. "You're going to march in there and sell those women some booty gear."

"Heidi?" I heard a soft knock on the door and a tinge of panic in Willow's voice. "Everything okay?"

I opened the door and stood eye to eye with my hostess. My smile was shaky. "I'm ready. Lead me to the Colosseum."

ⓔ ⓢ ⓔ

All right, so I wasn't a gladiator and they were significantly more pleasant than hungry lions waiting to tear me from limb to limb. In fact, things got off to a good, if rocky, start.

"Hi," I said to the group. Willow had gathered everyone in chairs and couches that formed a semicircle around me. "Thank you for coming to my first party as a Solomon's Closet consultant." I could feel an invisible puppeteer holding up the strings to keep my grin in place. "It is my goal today to help you ladies feel beautiful in your own skin. Solomon's Closet wants women of faith to feel comfortable and sexy in their own bedrooms. Or on the living room couch. Or the kitchen floor."

Someone may have laughed at my joke but I didn't notice because Laura Ingalls was hanging up her coat in the entryway behind the group. I shot a look to Willow, who gave a miniscule shrug as if to say, "Maybe she has sex, too."

What had I been thinking to entrust the invitation list to a woman who, in her words, hadn't felt "frisky" for half a decade?

"Show us what you've got, Heidi," Shelly said from her place on a love seat. "I'm in the mood for love, baby." Her chortle was met with a few embarrassed giggles.

Apparently First Lutheran was going to be a tougher nut to crack than the Pentecostals.

"Well," I said, clearing my throat, "we've got a little of everything." I turned to the nearest hat box and opened it up. Thongs. Too much (or too little) too soon. Box number two held nighties. I reached for a satin babydoll with two tiny bows by the straps. "This, for example, is sweet and pretty but still comfortable to sleep in."

I held the terra cotta–colored teddy up to Neesha's cappuccino-with-cream skin. Someone murmured appreciatively. That someone was not Laura Ingalls.

She cleared her throat from the back of the room. "Do you have anything more *modest?*" she asked as I began passing out the summer catalog.

I looked at her for a moment. Her small chin jutted out in righteous defiance.

"Well," I said, "I'm sure we can find something that would fit any taste. Solomon's Closet really tries to accommodate a wide spectrum of comfort levels. . . ." I trailed off, glancing at Willow with widened eyes. Help me out here, sister.

"Right," Willow sputtered, taking the cue. "I, for one, am interested in the silk pajamas on page twenty-two." She turned to Laura hopefully. "Perfect even for a girl who isn't getting any action."

The room erupted in laughter.

Laura sat up in her chair, pursing her thin lips.

Willow was bright red. "Not that *you* aren't getting any. I mean, *I'm* certainly not because I'm single, mostly —" She looked up at me from the miserable pit she was digging.

"And the point, of course," I said, "is that no matter your marital status, we all can use something to remind us that we are beautiful women." I took a breath. "Created by God," I added, throwing a fully clothed smile in Laura's direction. I could see the top of her French twist as she bowed her head to peruse the catalog. Or perhaps to pray for my soul.

Pockets of conversation had sprung up, the women busy discussing the catalog. I decided to take the opportunity to refill my glass of water. Willow met me by the fruit bowl.

"You're doing great," she whispered, reaching for a carafe of iced tea.

"You think so?" I looked at her anxiously, brushing a stray curl out of my eyes.

"Yes," she said. "If you can stop your hostess from insulting people's sex lives, you might even make some money." She shook her head in self-reprimand. "Sorry about that."

"Are you kidding? When this is all over, I'll join you in wild laughter."

Willow's eyes sparkled. "I'll bring the wine."

"Hush," I said, starting back toward the group. The noise volume was quickly on the rise. In fact, I had to summon my teacher voice to be heard over the din. "Does anyone have any questions?"

Mary, Willow's next-door neighbor, asked about the return policy.

I nodded. "You're welcome to return any item for merchandise credit, as long as you take care of shipping costs."

"If you're wondering about sizes," Shelly announced to the group, "I've always found smaller is better when it comes to this kind of thing." Boy, had I underestimated the Lutherans. Give 'em a catalogue and some croissants, and these ladies were on fire. It took a good ten seconds for the laughter from Shelly's joke to die down.

"Look at this, ladies." Neesha had been sifting through the items in one of my hat boxes. She held up a zebra-print corset with garters attached. She read the tag. "The Lion and Lamb Animal Print Collection. I'm buying this, girls, 'cause you *know* who's the lion and who's the lamb in my house."

At this point I was sure the raspberry liqueur had not baked out of Lupe's pastries. Molly asked for a vote on which would be better for her figure: a blue and yellow floral bra set or a kelly green nightie with "Sassy" embroidered across the rear. Unable to choose, she told me to put her down for both.

Shelly, against all the rules of the universe, insisted on trying on a thong outside her clothes, Nora style. I turned my head, trying to salvage for her whatever shred of dignity she still had. But I was the only one. The women hooted and hollered as Shelly turned in circles for the full—very full—effect.

And then, in the presence of God and all those witnesses, Laura Ingalls Wilder unearthed a side of her I wasn't even sure Almanzo had seen.

The room was still coming down from the Shelly incident and was the quietest it had been since my introductory spiel. Perfect conditions, in other words, for us to hear Laura from the back of the room.

"Now, this is *hot*," she said.

In slow motion, the women turned in their chairs, disbelief already registering on some of their faces. Laura stood up from her chair, holding against her a black lace unitard with plunging neck and back lines. I believe my mouth was open. This little number was one I'd almost left at home, assuming no one this side of Sixth Avenue would be interested in purchasing it for their own. Number one, though I was supposed to love everything Solomon's Closet offered, this thing was unequivocally the ugliest piece of lingerie I'd ever seen. Two, it had crotch snaps. And three, it was called "Jezebel's Secret Weapon," which was not only giving unadulterated literary license to a tragic biblical story, but was also uninspired marketing.

Laura loved it. She started moving in a way that suggested she was dancing, though I might have missed it. Neesha, however, had a better eye for this sort of thing and piped in with a chant of "You go, girl. Get your groove on. You work it. You own it." Laura continued her freestyle interpretation, even kicking off her leather clogs to really "work it."

Unfathomable.

Laura ended up being the big spender that afternoon, Jezebel's Secret Weapon only the beginning. My first Solomon's Closet party and I grossed seven hundred dollars. My own check, of course, was significantly smaller, but I felt good and was grateful to Willow for assisting with my debut.

"It was worth it to see sexual liberation hit First Lutheran's Moms' Group," she said afterward. I was helping her bring glasses and plates to the kitchen. "I must say, the whole experience struck me as very healthy, albeit with a twinge of *The Twilight Zone*. That *dance*," she said, shaking her head. "And to think I was worried I'd offended her by unintentionally suggesting her sex life had dried up."

I giggled, rubbing the back of my neck with my hand. "If it was before, it won't be when she gets her order in the mail." Willow walked with me to the door. "Are you sure you don't want me to stay and clean up?"

She shook her head and gave me a hug. "I'm not even going to do it today. I have a date to get ready for." She pulled away and started to dance. "I'm on it, I'm groovy—"

"Get your groove *on*, hippie," I corrected, shaking my head as I opened the door. "Just remain pure, okay? I can't handle another church-lady shocker this month."

"No worries," she said, still working it out. "David hasn't even kissed me yet." She began to freestyle chant. "Too shy, too quiet, too scared, he's a gentleman."

When I pulled away from the curb, she was still on her front porch, hands in the air and breaking out all her best moves.

chapter/fifteen

A few days later, Nora and I stood on the threshold of our front door, mouths agape as July's life-sapping humidity slithered into our cool foyer.

"I don't want to hear it," Micah said, scuffing a polished wingtip by kicking it against the door frame.

"Wow," I said. "You look, um, really nice."

Nora took a step closer and squinted up into Micah's face. After a pause, she announced, "It's him, Mom! It's Micah!"

There stood our disillusioned, antiestablishment Micah in a gray pinstriped suit, pale blue oxford, and tie. His shoes were free of holes, though I'd glimpsed bright green socks when he kicked the door. But the most startling transformation was the hair, which was slicked back into a neat ponytail.

Micah looked like a Young Republican. A miserable one, but one nonetheless.

He rolled his eyes. "May I please come in? I need to take off my noose." He'd already loosened the red and blue striped necktie so that the knot hung well below the second button on his shirt. I moved aside to let him in. "Thanks," he mumbled.

"Micah, are you wearing Old Spice?" I asked, shutting the door behind us.

"Please, Mrs. Elliott," Micah said, his eyes imploring.

"Don't make this any rougher than it is. I had a job interview, okay?"

"An interview, eh?" I said, my mouth unable to resist a small smile. I checked myself and went somber once more. "Where?"

"At the cell phone store in the mall. They're looking for communication consultants."

"Fancy," I said. "I hear consultants can charge super high rates because the rest of us don't know any better." I glimpsed Nora in her room, tossing all the clothes out of her drawers.

"Yeah, well, that must be a different kind of consultant because I'd still only make eleven bucks an hour."

"Eleven? Good gravy, Micah." I was making a second pass through the kitchen in search of my car keys, starting to curse myself again for not investing in a key homing device. Maybe a pigeon. "Eleven an hour is pretty good, isn't it? I remember I made four seventy-five an hour at my first job. Hostess at The Koffee Kup."

"The what?"

I entered the living room. Micah was smirking.

"The Koffee Kup. It used to be on the corner of Van Dorn and Miner's Road. Cute little café, calico curtains, homemade cinnamon rolls."

"Dang," Micah said, snapping his fingers. "I forgot to look for a *cute* place to work. What was I thinking?"

"Awfully sassy with your *current* employer, aren't you?" I said, one eyebrow raised.

Micah grinned. "I'd say you were right, but the pay's not that great anyway."

Nora entered the room and ran to tackle Micah at the

legs. She was dressed in one of her favorite Micah-inspired ensembles: black turtleneck (in July), black corduroy skirt, black tights, and red mini high-tops given to her by the Young Republican himself.

Micah growled and lifted Nora horizontally, using her as his air guitar. "Bad pay, oh yeah," he intoned, Nora's giggles reaching a feverish pitch with each "strum." He droned on, "But the benefits rock, oh yeah." I wouldn't have called it singing, but then again, concerned churchgoers had been known to turn around in their pews following the doxology to ask if I was sick.

"Yessss," I cheered after locating a spare set of keys in a winter coat pocket. "I'm off, you two."

Micah let Nora fall onto the couch. Her red chucks kicked over her head. "Any instructions?"

"Just a snack sometime while I'm gone. I shouldn't be long, unless the doctor's office is running late." I kissed Nora's flushed cheek. "Bye, babe."

"Bye, Mommy," she said, scrambling away from my kiss. "Micah, I want to be a guitar again."

He caught her as she leaped into his arms. Already having cast aside the suit jacket, tie, and shoes, he was starting to look much more like himself. Slicked hair was out of its ponytail holder and had begun a cowlicked migration around his face. "See ya," he said, flashing a grin.

"You didn't take out your tongue ring?" I turned the doorknob and pulled.

"Dude, Mrs. Elliott," he said, holding Nora upside down by her ankles. "Can't I retain one shred of autonomy in front of The Man?"

I could hear Nora trying to sing along to vintage Pearl Jam as I shut the door.

℮ ℈ ℮

It's an interesting thing, the Pap smear. Each year I tried to fake myself out, convince myself that it really wasn't that bad. This line of reasoning made perfect sense when it was placed on the Scale of Horrific Human Experiences. Sudan, for example, was bad. Katrina was bad. Tsunami, bad. I recognized these statements to be true and encouraged myself to cowboy up, even as I put on my paper gown and waited on the cold exam table, feet in stirrups, staring at the fluorescent lights. It's no big deal, I reminded myself, starting to shiver. I've birthed an eight-pound baby, for Pete's sake. Much larger things have passed through that canal than a cotton swab.

I heard a soft knock on the door and then "Hellohello, Heidihowareyou?" Dr. Kahn came in, trailed by a blonde nurse with a name tag reading Marcie. As only an OB/GYN can do, Dr. Kahn breezed right past the stirrups and the picture they framed and arrived at my side to shake my hand.

"I'm fine, Dr. Kahn. And you?"

"Finejustfine, justfine," she said, smiling. Years in an overworked medical practice had stuck Dr. Kahn's speech on permanent fast-forward. She nodded at me and patted my arm rapidly. Her dark eyes, set above defined cheekbones, flickered with warmth. I'd found it best if one got on well with one's OB, considering the power they wielded in instrumentation alone. And I liked Dr. Kahn. Now in her early sixties, she had been my gynecologist before morphing into my obstetrician, and after all those years under her care, the only thing that made me a tinge uncomfortable was that she frothed at the mouth. Purely accidental, mind you, and only in the throes of passionate discourse concerning women's reproductive health, but it happened, and I couldn't help but feel a bit awkward.

"And Nora?" she asked, running her hands under the strong spray of the exam room faucet. She worked up an antibacterial lather before rinsing and slamming the handle down. Dr. Kahn couldn't have tipped the scales much beyond one hundred pounds, but her biceps were intimidating. She'd once told me about growing up with four brothers in New Delhi and how she'd learned to survive as the runt of the litter. I saw a black digital runner's watch peeking from the sleeve of her lab coat, and my mind flashed to a child version of Dr. Kahn outrunning a group of boys pursuing her down banyan-lined streets. "I'll bet she's getting to be a big girl, yes? Wants to go to school already?"

"She just turned four."

"Four, mygoodnessgracious. Four years since you had that very long labor, do you remember?"

"Hard to forget," I said, watching Dr. Kahn unwrap the sterilized speculum.

"Okay, Heidi," she said, settling on a stool at the foot of the table. "You may feel a bit of discomfort."

Tell me about it, sister.

I breathed deeply. I looked at Marcie's face for distraction. She appeared to be right around fifteen years old. If a woman has to feel old and decrepit, isn't it salt in the wound to feel that way while getting swabbed?

"Woo," I said on a sharp intake of breath.

"All done," Dr. Kahn said, handing the speculum and swab to Marcie before snapping off her latex gloves. She offered a hand to help me sit up. "That will be all, Marcie."

Marcie turned in her white Birkenstocks and left the room, closing the door quietly on her way out.

"We'll send the sample out to the lab, but I'd say everything looks normal, Heidi," Dr. Kahn said when we were alone. Her brow was knit into a line of attentive concentration. "Marcie said you are concerned about your failure to conceive."

I nodded, a lump forming in my throat.

"How long have you and Jake been trying?"

"Around five months."

Dr. Kahn raised her eyebrows. "I would say this is premature to be concerned. We don't start to worry until you have been trying for one year with no success."

"A year? But with Nora I got pregnant right away."

Dr. Kahn nodded. "Right. This is very common."

"What is?"

"Secondary infertility."

"Infertility?" I said. My heart had taken a nosedive to the soles of Dr. Kahn's Crocs. My voice became small. "I'm infertile?"

"Not irreversibly." Dr. Kahn hunched toward me, her eyes bright. I could feel a froth coming on. "Heidi, many women, for reasons we don't fully understand, experience difficulty conceiving their second child. Sometimes infertility is a result of stress, physical or emotional or both."

"I don't feel stressed," I said, eager to defend my ability to procreate. "I mean, I've started working part-time—"

"Exactly," Dr. Kahn said. One point for her! "Sometimes

new situations can bring on stress, even hidden stress we haven't yet acknowledged." She took out a little cloth to dab the sides of her mouth. "But even without stress or outside factors, women's bodies change. There are a multitude of conditions that can cause infertility. Unfavorable levels of progesterone, estrogen, glucose, a malfunctioning thyroid. . . . The list is really quite extensive. Are you ovulating?"

"I think so."

"Let's see your chart."

I looked at her blankly, certain I would not be getting an A in AP Ovulation. "I don't exactly have one."

Dr. Kahn nodded quickly. "That's where we'll begin. I want you to keep a calendar of when you ovulate—you can use either the basal temperature method or ovulation predictor kits—when your periods occur, for how long, and if there's any change in flow."

I could imagine Jake's graying face at the words "change in flow." "Okay," I said. "But won't that take awhile?"

Dr. Kahn rose and walked to the sink. She flipped on the faucet handles and began sudsing up again. I was beginning to suspect an OCD issue. "It may seem like a long time, but I'll need to verify a pattern of menstruation and ovulation before taking any other measures."

"Measures like what? In vitro?"

Dr. Kahn pumped twice on the econo-size lotion dispenser. "Nonono, notyetHeidi. First we would do blood work to see if anything raises a red flag. If there is an issue with ovulation, we have some medication that can help jumpstart your ovaries."

I winced, picturing my jumper cables on a dead battery in the middle of winter.

"IVF is an option, but we won't cross that bridge for many moons." She laughed at what must have been a joke. I supposed OBs had to get their kicks, too. Why not with puns on moon phases?

"Heidi, do you have any more questions?" Dr. Kahn stood in front of me, her head tilted slightly as she looked into my eyes.

"So for now, I just keep track of what's happening down there." The paper gown I wore was open in back and I shivered from the cold air on my skin.

"Ha!" Dr. Kahn's laugh really was that one syllable. "Ha ha! 'Down there.' That's right, Heidi. Tell me *what's up down there*." She pointed up and down to accompany her words.

Geez. It was time for Dr. Kahn to venture beyond the waiting room.

"Okay, then," I said, smiling a wobbly smile. "Thanks, Dr. Kahn."

"Ofcourseofcourseofcourse," she said. "Say hello to Nora and Jake, please. And call us anytime, okay, Heidi? Don't worry, eh? We will figure out what's going on 'down there.'" More inappropriate laughter and she was gone.

I sat on the exam table a moment, hugging myself for warmth. My insides were shaking. "Everything looks normal," I said, trying to reassure myself. I hopped down from the crinkly paper and untied the robe at the neck.

Ghastly word, I thought as I pulled on my clothes. Secondary, primary—in whatever form, infertility was not something I'd wanted to hear.

chapter/sixteen

"At least we have a plan, right?"

My husband, the optimist. "Yes, we have a plan." I sighed into my cell phone, glad Jake couldn't see my rolling eyes. At times I found it exhausting to share a bed with a male version of Pollyanna.

Not quite ready to face my real life, I was making a detour by way of the bookstore before heading home. Parker Books was a favorite haunt for college students, artsy folk, and bibliophiles of all ages. In the era of the megabookstore, Parker had managed to stay afloat by offering a wide selection of books and magazines, many of the titles off the radars of larger chain stores. The menagerie of printed materials made for lively perusing, both of books and of the people who read them.

I lowered my voice as I ambled past self-help, scanning the spines as I walked. "Jake, did you know there's a book called *Sweet and Golden: Using Organic Honey to Reclaim the Goddess Within?*"

"Sounds sexual."

"No it doesn't."

"Sure it does. What do you think pent-up goddesses do when they're reclaimed?"

"You're a pathetic individual."

Over Jake's laughter, I heard a familiar voice near the cash register. I peeked over a large-print copy of *Stop Hating Yourself* to catch a glimpse.

"I don't see how it's my fault if the book was misshelved," Kylie was saying to the clerk, a college-aged student who looked like she was about to cry.

"Gotta go," I whispered into the phone. "Call you later." I snapped my phone shut and crept into biographies to have a closer look. My view allowed for a side profile of the standoff. Kylie stood with shoulders back and chin raised, glowering at the girl behind the counter. Her hair was pulled back in a sleek ponytail. I'd seen the tailored black sundress with white stitching in the window of a shop downtown and knew it had never visited the clearance rack. She'd pushed wide black sunglasses to the top of her head and had folded her hands on the countertop. Her ring finger was dwarfed by an insanely large diamond glinting in the canister lights.

The shop girl, whose name tag read either Jane or the less likely but more apt Zane, wore a faded orange cardigan over a Sex Pistols T-shirt. Jane/Zane's hair, its original color known only to her mother, looked like it had been through many a metamorphosis but at present was washed in bright red dye with stripes of blue. She was chewing on the inside of her lower lip, hand placed protectively on the book lying between her and Kylie.

"I'm sorry, ma'am, but this book is not on sale. Someone must have picked it up while shopping and didn't put it back on the proper shelf." There was a faint tremor in Jane/Zane's voice, incongruous with the hair, but she was holding her own keeping Kylie's gaze.

"Well," Kylie said with a huff. "Maybe I should speak to a manager." She scanned the room.

"I *am* the manager," the girl said, looking none too pleased about her illustrious title.

I squinted my eyes to read the title of the book in question. Standing on my tiptoes, I could just make out the words on the cover. I gulped. *Why Jesus Wants You to Be Rich.*

"Kylie," I called, moving quickly out of biographies toward the register.

She turned toward me with a smile so wide it exposed her bottom row of teeth. "Heidi, hello! How are you?"

I glanced at Jane/Zane. "Fine, thanks." I nodded toward the book. "I don't mean to interrupt. Go ahead and finish. I'll wait." I took a step aside and pulled a greeting card off a rotating rack by the door.

I couldn't hear what Kylie said in a lowered voice, but Jane/Zane's face was a mix of confusion and relief. She rang up Kylie's purchase while I made my way through a vertical row of sympathy cards.

"Did someone lose a loved one?" Kylie asked when she joined me. Her face was drawn in concern.

"What? Oh, no," I said, sliding a picture of white orchids back into a slot. "Just looking."

"Hmm," Kylie said, nodding. "Well. I saw the numbers for your first party. Not bad at all for a first time out. You should be pleased."

"Thank you," I said. "My friends were very kind to come."

Kylie arched her brows. "And *you* were kind to provide them with an exceptional product." She pointed her index finger at my nose. "Don't you start thinking you're indebted to them. Those women had a life-expanding experience and you were the one to provide it."

"Right," I mumbled, locking eyes with Jane/Zane, who was watching us from behind the corner. She immediately averted her gaze and began straightening a display of book-marks. "Well, I should finish my shopping," I said. I looked at my watch. "Never anger the babysitter, right?" My laugh sounded hollow.

Kylie didn't seem to notice. "I'll call you later this week. You're due for dinner at the Zimmermans'."

The way she said this made me think I was supposed to jump up and bump chests with a passerby or do an Arsenio Hall bark. "Great," I said, settling for a toothy smile and a sorority-girl shrug. "I'll look forward to it."

After a quick wave, she retrieved her sunglasses from the top of her head with manicured fingers and pushed open the glass door, letting in a gush of humidity as she left.

I plucked an "In Your Time of Sorrow" card from the stack and took it to the counter.

"Find everything okay?" Jane/Zane asked, her eyes trained on mine.

"Yes, thank you," I said, hoping my smile said "warmth," "kindness," "loves hourly wage earners."

"Two sixty-three." At closer range, I could see her name tag. I'd been close, but her name was actually Lanie. She flipped a strand of blue to her back and waited as I took out a five.

"I'm sorry about that," I said in a lowered voice, nodding my head toward where Kylie and I had stood talking.

Lanie looked at me warily. "You don't need to apologize," she said.

"Yes, I do," I said, thinking of *Why Jesus Wants You To Be Rich*.

"Why, is she your sister or something?"

"Not exactly," I said, though I'd told Nora just last week that the song "We Are Family" meant we were all God's children. Poetic license, I knew, but I believed in teachable moments.

Lanie shrugged and handed me my change. "Don't worry about it. I've found that with people like her, it's usually not about the book."

I nodded slowly. "Wise girls, you Parker Books types."

Lanie allowed herself a small smile. "Have a nice day."

"You, too," I said, and I meant it.

© ᗡ ©

After putting Nora to bed that night, I found Jake sitting bug-eyed at the computer.

"Hey," I said, sitting down on the futon I'd had since college. We'd covered the mattress with a pale green sheet in an attempt to mask the wild Bermuda print that lay underneath. It had been a screaming bargain for a poor college student willing to look beyond questionable aesthetics.

"Hi," Jake said belatedly. My husband was not adept at multitasking. In that moment, he was in the "Computer" box, which meant the "Conversing with Heidi" box was shoved toward the back of the closet somewhere, probably between "Sharing Real Emotion" and "Watching A Movie That

Doesn't Involve Blowing People Up." Curiously, the "Sex" box remained open and readily accessible no matter what the hour, the weather, or the status of the rest of the closet.

"Yes!" Jake shouted, making me jump and then slap him on the arm as a reminder that his child was sleeping.

"Wake her up and you're stuck with her."

"Sorry," he said, eyes glued to the screen. "Heidi, listen to this: four nights at the Westin in Bangkok, airfare, and rental car for six ninety-nine a person."

I looked heavenward. "Jake."

"Airport taxes included." He did a fist pump.

"Uh-huh. And a rental car."

"Exactly! *And* a car."

"Because you never know when you'll need a maroon Ford Taurus in Bangkok."

Jake continued staring at the screen, muttering to himself. "Offer good through the twenty-first, which is . . . tomorrow. Whew. Just made it."

"Jake."

"Hmm?"

"I need to check my e-mail."

No response. Men are interesting, aren't they? If I'd said, "Jake, I've always wanted to visit Bangkok, and my calendar's clear tomorrow," Jake would have snapped his little neck turning from the screen to give me his full attention. And if I'd been naked when I spoke, he would have needed immediate medical attention. But since my words did not coincide with his game plan, they bounced off the office walls, unheard.

"Jake," I said, volume up a notch.

"Yeah? What'd you say?"

"I need to check my e-mail." I enunciated like an American tourist talking to a foreigner.

"Okay," he said over a frenzy of mouse clicking. "I'm finished." He logged out and spun around in his office chair to face me. "But seriously, Heidi," he said. His face was somber enough for a funeral. "Think about Bangkok." He nodded slowly, perhaps willing me to taste the Pad Thai that awaited us.

"Seriously. I will." I nodded right along with him and matched his grave expression.

"Love you," he said, jumping up and planting one on me. "Tell me when you're done. I'll just run a few more numbers before bed."

I tapped the mouse with my finger as I waited for my account to open, then began wading through the twenty-six new messages, deleting all those in the bulk folder and not even opening half the ones in my in-box before they were zapped. Most of the remaining messages were related to Solomon's Closet: pep talks and motivational case studies by Kylie, updates on the catalog, order notices from the three parties I'd hosted. I replied to an invitation to a couples' dinner at the Zimmerman home that coming Friday. Kylie also asked me to start compiling a list of women I thought might benefit from selling SC and to gather their contact information. Ah yes, I thought. Heading in for the kill. I made a note in my day planner about the dinner and my homework assignment.

Solomon's Closet and bulk mailings out of the way, I settled in for the few personal e-mails waiting to be read. There were three, all of them from Annie. I read the least recent first. It was short:

From: anniebananie@wordlink.com
To: amorcita@springdale.net
Subject: Please call the Sergeant

H-

Would you mind calling Becca at the office and asking
her to check the office e-mail account? I've been trying
to get through for a few days but something's not
working right. Maybe she hasn't paid the monthly fee
to AOL?

Thanks. Off to some Italian rock concert tonight with
James. He's hot AND he's hip. Can you believe it?

Will write later-

A

I jotted a note to myself to call Becca the next day and
opened the second message.

From: anniebananie@wordlink.com
To: amorcita@springdale.net
Subject: S.O.S.

Heidi-

I'm writing at a ridiculous hour, but I can't sleep
anyway. Maybe I should just call you but I think it'll do
me good to write this out.

James and I had a horrible fight tonight, our first. I'm
drained and I don't know what to think about it. So I'm
writing you for sound advice.

We were standing in line to get into the concert I
wrote about this afternoon. James had left to use the
restroom and I was holding our place in line. He was
gone forever, and I started to get worried, thinking
maybe he'd gotten hurt or lost. I know, a little irrational,
but even after a few months here and no problems, I

can't ignore that we are Americans visiting a foreign country and that some people don't feel great about the U.S. these days. Not to mention, do Italians like black people? Provincial thinking, maybe, but I'm new at both Italy and interracial dating, so cut me some slack.

Just as I was about to give up my place in line and go looking for him, I spotted James in the crowd. There were thousands of people at this concert and the lobby was jam-packed. James was standing very close to this willowy, gorgeous Italian woman with long dark hair and a body that would not quit, in any culture. I stared at them. He leaned in to hear her better, and she kept putting her hand on his arm, his shoulder, maybe even his backside, for all I know. My view was partially blocked.

My initial joy that he wasn't mugged and blooding in some narrow alleyway lasted about a nanosecond with THAT visual image to contend with. After a few more minutes and lots of cheek kissing with Sophia Loren (in her prime, not "Grumpy Old Men"), he strolled back over to me. I was furious, hurt, embarrassed, but it came out all furious. We argued in line, like the repressed Americans we are, quietly and not really looking at each other. The concert was miserable, even though the music was great. Afterward, as we walked back to my hotel, we sparred, this time not so quietly. He insisted Hot Italian Girl was an old friend from the last time he worked in Milan, years ago, and that their meeting was a pleasant surprise and nothing more. Lots of words about different levels of cultural comfort and physical touch, blah, blah, blah. But I stayed angry. And I'm still angry, only now I've added a layer of self-loathing that I'm still angry.

Am I a middle school girl?

Help me, wise married one.

Love and miss you. Give a kiss to Nora and tell her

boys have cooties. It's safer that way.

A

I started a reply immediately.

From: amorcita@springdale.net
To: anniebananie@wordlink.com
Subject: RE: S.O.S.

Annie,

You are not a middle school girl. I knew you when you were, though, and I must say you look much better without headgear.

You are not being unreasonable. How were/are you supposed to know Hot Italian Girl was platonic in her dealings with James? What if he was harboring secret feelings for her and all you could do was stand idly by, in line to see the boy band or whatever, and wonder? And why didn't he bring H.I.G. (Hot Italian Girl) over to meet you if everything was so innocent?

These are perfectly justifiable questions. The thing is, you barely know this guy, Annie. I mean, maybe it feels like you do, but you've only known each other a short time, relatively speaking. Relative to the life span of a tortoise, for example (87,942 years). Or relative to the age of the Uffizi in Florence (see? I'm trying to be culturally relevant). In "love time," it probably feels like you've known each other forever, but it's okay to remember you're still new at this relationship. You are still totally within sound thinking to be wary when you see James hanging on other women, willowy and otherwise.

I'd be cautious. You probably don't want to hear that right now, but I'm the old married one here, remember? True, I kissed Jake before I knew his name, but that was for money. That didn't come out quite right. . . . The point is, you are not overreacting and you should feel the freedom to take this whole thing nice and slow.

At least until I meet him and give you my blessing.

Okay, okay. So he won't exactly need to ask me for your hand, but you get my point. Don't you?

I love you, Annie. Walk softly and carry a big stick, unless that's illegal in Europe, in which case you might have to carry an umbrella. Just make sure this James character is careful with your heart.

Nora sends a fierce hug.

Heidi

I sighed as I clicked "send." The travails of new love. How much more complicated when dating in an Italian vacuum with no best friend to sift through the riffraff. I clicked on the last message, starting to feel the weight of a long day seep into my body. The last letter was short.

From: anniebananie@wordlink.com
To: amorcita@springdale.net
Subject: False alarm

H-

Ignore last e-mail. James showed up at my hotel at four a.m., unable to sleep as well and wanting to talk. We did, he's wonderful, and I'm happily exhausted.

Don't know why I ever worried.

I'm headed to bed. We're meeting for dinner. Hope J makes it through his workday on basically no sleep.

Your friend and the luckiest woman in Italy,

Annie

Right. Well, at least I didn't give her my top ten reasons of why this romance was doomed to failure. I'd wait to see if James's philandering became a recurrent problem before sending that off.

I shut down the computer and turned off the office lights. Back upstairs, I could hear Jake's electric toothbrush from our bathroom.

"Hiwooeih?" he said through foam.

"Sorry?"

Jake nodded toward the sink.

"Go ahead and spit." I pulled off my shirt and shorts and retrieved my pj's from behind my pillow.

"So what's the word? Are we going to Bangkok?" Jake climbed in next to me. He took a look at my ratty tank top and boxer shorts. "And why aren't you doing more market research with Solomon's Closet stuff? I thought I'd get way more mileage out of this."

I rolled on my side to turn off the bedside lamp. "No on the Bangkok and later on the market research. I should start ovulating in a few days. Save your energy."

"What makes you think I don't have energy to spare, woman?" Jake ran his hands down the curve of my side.

"G'night," I said, burrowing my face into my pillow.

Jake stayed plastered against my side and initiated what in educational circles would be termed *inappropriate touching*.

"Heidi," he said into my ear. "Remember me?"

"Vaguely," I said. I inched farther away, teetering on the edge of the bed.

"Hey," he said, pulling my shoulder toward him so that we faced each other. "What's going on?"

"Nothing," I said, closing my eyes. "I'm just really tired. I witnessed a disturbing incident involving Kylie in the bookstore today, Annie's literally a world away and may be involved with a total player, and my husband is badgering me for sex right before launching into a week of intentional baby making. I'm selling lingerie for my business, but I feel like having sex to get pregnant is becoming my real job."

Jake rolled onto his back, away from me. "I didn't know having sex with me stressed you out so much."

And now, my friends, we had entered the minefield of Injured Male Pride. Dangerous, shark-infested waters, and yet I jumped in without even a wet suit. "Jake, give me a break. This is not about you. I'm just tired, okay?"

The silence draped over us, accompanied by an orchestra of cicadas outside our window.

I fell asleep to their music.

chapter/seventeen

A week later I sat at the dining room table, engulfed by paper-work and UPS boxes, trying to sort out an ordering mix-up from my second Solomon's Closet party. After my debut at Willow's, Lori and Daniela had pulled together a group of neighborhood women and hosted a party at Lori's house. Those women had wound up being even rowdier than the Pentecostals. Louise Angelo, for example, glorious in a magenta and orange silk kimono, had given a lengthy dissertation on her interpretation of the Kama Sutra, highlighting the bene-fits of stretching before "making whoopee" (her words). The evening was utterly exhausting, I must say. And to top it off, two of the women had paid incorrect amounts, one woman was missing her order altogether, and another had called to see if she could change the sizing on everything she'd bought containing spandex.

And as accompaniment to this mayhem, Nora was trying out for the debate team.

"Mom, you said we could go to the zoo today." She was hopping on one foot in circles around the table.

"I know, honey, but Mommy has to do things for work."

Nora hopped by and sent a jumble of papers fluttering to the floor. "What's your work called?"

"Nora, you just bumped all those papers off the table. What do you say?" I leaned over and began picking them up.

"Sorry, Mom." She stopped hopping and crouched down to help me but I'd finished by the time she'd gathered three papers.

"Never mind. I've got it." Calculator cleared once more, I started over on the first invoice.

"Can we go to the zoo, Mom?" Nora commenced her jumping. She wore moon boots, a swimsuit, and a cowboy hat.

"Can't, Norie." I scribbled a new total at the bottom of the first invoice.

"You sell underwear, right, Mom?" She was alternating skipping and hopping.

"Well, yes. I do." So to speak. Not exactly My Little Pony cotton briefs, but there would be time to explain that later.

"That's what I told my teacher at Sunday school."

I looked up from the calculator. "You told your teacher at Sunday school that Mommy sells underwear?"

Nora nodded. "And bras. And underwear made out of strings."

Excellent. "What did your teacher say?" I scanned my mental Rolodex, trying to picture who'd taught Nora's Sunday school last weekend.

"She said she thought you were a mom. But I told her you weren't a mom anymore. Now you sell underwear."

Kick me while I'm down, I thought, watching Nora walk on all fours around the perimeter of the room. She rose abruptly and knocked her head on the underside of the table.

I jumped off my chair and pulled my wailing daughter to

me. "Are you all right, sweet pea?" I checked the red bump swelling on the top of her head.

She buried her face into my neck. "Not yet," she whimpered.

"Poor lovey," I said into her hair. I sat cross-legged with her on my lap, rocking her back and forth. She inhaled shakily, moaned on the exhale. I wrapped her curls around my fingers. "I'm still a mom, peanut."

"You are?" She pulled an arm across her runny nose.

"I'll always be your mom, no matter what."

Nora rocked with me, relaxing in my grip. "A mom who sells underwear and strings?"

"Right." Forgive me, God, for teaching my child what a thong is before she's learned the Apostles' Creed.

"Can we go to the zoo, Mom?" Nora looked up. She pushed her hair out of her eyes and put a small hand on each of my shoulders. "I think we need a break."

I smiled. "I think you're right."

Nora jumped up, already trying to wriggle out of her swimsuit. "Let's go to the peacocks first," she said, cawing on her way to her room.

I took a last look at my stack of invoices before following her, picking up moon boots and a cowboy hat on the way.

ⓔ ◌ ⓔ

That evening I hobbled out of our bedroom and toward our front entryway, one high heel on and one in my hand. My hand made it to the knob on the third ring of the doorbell.

"Hi, Micah," I said, pushing open the screen door against a

strong wind. The forecast had called for thunderstorms beginning late, and the charcoal sky supported the weatherman's
claims. "Come in."

Micah edged past me into the house. "It's gonna pour."

Quarter-size drops of rain had begun to splatter the brick
sidewalk leading to the front porch. I shut the door behind us
and called for Nora.

Nora came walking slowly out of her room, chin upturned
and avoiding my gaze. "Hello, Micah," she said. Unable to
resist, she stole a glance in my direction and scowled.

"Hi, Sass." Micah turned to me and said under his breath,
"Mother-daughter angst already?"

I rolled my eyes. Nora's back was turned toward me as she
escaped to the living room. "She's mad at me."

"Won't let her go to prom with a senior?" Micah grinned.

"Close. I took her to the zoo today but I was basically on
the phone the whole time for work."

"I see," Micah said, nodding slowly. "The cell phone is the
worst enemy of today's cohesive family."

I stared at him. "Where did you hear that?"

He shrugged. "Made it up, thank you very much. Don't
think I'm not in touch with the corrosion of human interaction in today's America." A wild Lambada melody rang from
a deep pocket in his baggy jeans.

I bit my lip and raised an eyebrow, holding back a
chortle.

He pulled out his cell phone and checked the caller ID.
"Sorry," he said, a half smile playing on his lips. "I have to
take this."

"Certainly." I smiled and turned toward Jake, who'd

emerged from the bedroom, showered and spiffy. "Hello, hot husband." I kissed him on the lips. "You smell good."

"Dinner at an Avalon house requires cologne. We of the plebian class don't often get invitations to break bread with the high rollers."

"Just don't pick your teeth or spit on your hand before you shake, and you should stay under the radar."

"What about the fork issue?" He stood after lacing his dress shoes. I took him in: dark gray pinstriped suit, light blue shirt to match his eyes, blue tie with yellow polka dots. Black belt and shoes, shined for the occasion.

I pulled his tie toward me and lifted my face to his. I whispered in his ear, "Just move from the outside in and you'll be fine." I kissed his neck.

"Oh yeah, and we can talk about the forks later, heh heh." Jake moved his neck from side to side in a most disturbing white boy-dancing kind of way.

I laughed and wrapped my arms around him.

Micah cleared his throat.

We looked at our punk babysitter, who was nervously flipping his tongue ring back and forth.

"Hi, Micah," Jake said. "Don't let the unsavory married people scare you." He twirled me away from him and initiated what might have been a swing dance. "We don't get out enough."

Micah nodded slowly. "Right, Mr. Elliott. I never would have guessed."

I started in on bedtime instructions, but Micah interrupted me. "Mrs. Elliott, I've been here five times this week. I think I've got it."

I winced. "Five times?"

"Yep."

"I see. Well," I said, clasping and unclasping my purse. "We'll head out then." I walked to Nora's room, where I found her fiddling with the clock radio by her bed.

"We're off, Norie," I said. I sat down beside her and pulled her toward me.

She squirmed away. "I can't talk with you. You'll have to tell Bear if you have a message for me."

I sighed and grabbed Bear from his post by Nora's pillow. "Okay. Bear." Bear looked at me with blank button eyes, but I knew he was listening. "Bear, please tell Nora I'm very sorry about being on the phone at the zoo. Tell her I had to talk with all those boring people because I'm trying to do a good job at my work. But I'm still sorry because I'd much rather be with Nora than do anything else."

"Bear," Nora said, "tell Mommy that I don't like the zoo anyway."

I looked at Nora but kept holding on to Bear. "Maybe tomorrow we can try the park. And if you're good tonight, Bear, maybe you can come, too."

"And have a picnic?" Nora looked up from her radio.

"And have a picnic." I scooted toward Nora. "Do you forgive me, Norie?"

"Yes," she said, resting her head on my shoulder. "I forgive you, but I still have to put you in time-out." Her face was grave.

"I see," I said, nodding. "Would it be all right if my time-out was with Daddy at a dinner for grown-ups?"

"Probably," she said. "But you won't be able to have any fruit snacks."

"All right," I said, hugging her to me. "I love you, Norie."

"Love you, too." She kissed me on the cheek. "Can you tell Micah to come dance?" She pulled her radio onto her lap and turned up the volume. Prince blared "1999," and Nora slid off her bed and started to boogy. Her compromised musical gene pool had served her well thus far, as Micah's style of "dancing" looked more like convulsions than anything requiring a steady beat.

Micah and Jake met me halfway to the front door, and we tagged out for the evening, leaving Prince, a punk, and a princess to get their groove on in our absence.

chapter/eighteen

Jake let out a low whistle as we pulled into the circular driveway at the Zimmerman place.

"I tried to warn you," I said, flipping down the visor mirror
for one last check.

"This is bigger than my elementary school," Jake said.
He'd wedged his head between the top of the steering wheel
and the windshield for better gawking.

"Discretion, please. They could be looking out a
window."

Jake pulled out of his contortionist's pose. He coasted to a
stop behind two other cars, the right side of his mouth pulling
into a smile. "At least our smokin' wheels will fit right in."

I followed his gaze. The car at the front of the line was a
silver Mercedes convertible; directly before us sat a chocolate
brown Bentley. Both cars had discreet window stickers adver-
tising Solomon's Closet.

I slapped the dashboard of Jake's truck and said in my best
redneck growl, "Yeah, but who can haul a half ton of lumber
in a mud slide? Not those pansies."

Jake shook his head. "Maybe we should have taken the
Beast."

"And run the risk of stalling on the brick driveway, right

in front of the topiaries? Or having to park at a diagonal so they wouldn't notice the passenger's door is a different color than the rest of the car?"

"What are topiaries?"

"Let's go." I opened my door. The Civic would have made for a more ladylike exit, but Jake's truck was clean and all one color. Plus, it had twelve fewer years on the road than the Beast. I balanced one foot on the running board and stepped down to the driveway. I was wearing an outfit I'd purchased that afternoon at Burke's, Springdale's high-end department store. Not the best way to save money, impulse buying, but I'd panicked. When Kylie had called a few days prior to firm up the time for dinner, I'd asked what Jake and I should wear.

"Let's see . . ." she'd said. "How about formal? So seldom do we get a chance to dress up. It'll be fun!"

Spoken as a person who probably not only owned but actually used a strapless bra. I, however, had spent the summer wearing mostly jeans and capris, feeling really ambitious when I poked in some earrings. *Formal*, while music to Nora's ears, was an adjective that sent shivers down my spine. Something told me wearing my wedding dress with the open back wasn't really what Kylie was envisioning.

So I'd caved that afternoon and blown a large part of my third Solomon's Closet check on a cocktail dress I'd found at Burke's. The end-of-summer sale had saved me from taking out a home equity line of credit, but it was still pricey. The dress was a soft green that matched the lighter flecks in my eyes. The V-neck gave the optical illusion that I hadn't lost my cleavage in a lactating incident. Ruche in the bodice and a flare in the skirt just plain fooled onlookers into thinking I had curves in the right places. It was late August, so my arms and legs were tan enough to bare without injuring any retinas. I'd painted my toenails, which peeked through a pair of strappy heels.

Jake met me on the passenger side. He kissed me on the cheek. "You look nice."

I eyed him warily. "Thanks. You're being awfully polite. No lewd comments?"

He shrugged and took my arm. "I'm meeting your boss. I don't know what kind of woman she is, but most can't handle a full dosage of Jake Elliott on the first meeting."

We stepped up to the front door and rang the bell. The summer night air was a heady mix of the impending storm and the recently watered gardens that sprawled along the front of the house. "Those are topiaries," I said, pointing to the manicured trees gracing both sides of the entrance. They were lit with tiny white lights that twinkled in the descending purple dusk.

The door flew open with a *whoosh* that made me jump. Jake straightened abruptly, pulling his nose out of a topiary. A woman in her twenties wearing a gray and white maid's uniform greeted us. "Mr. and Mrs. Elliott?" Her voice lilted with the rhythm of a native Spanish speaker.

Jake held out his hand to shake. "Jake."

She looked surprised but offered her hand. "I am Marisa."

I smiled and shook. "Nice to meet you, Marisa. I'm Heidi."

Her brown eyes widened. "You said my name right," she said as she stepped aside to let us in.

Jake's head rested in an upward tilt, mouth open, as he got

his first glimpse of the Tabuchi.

"I lived in Ecuador for a year during college." I nudged Jake as Marisa led us past the staircase and down the center hallway.

"*Entonces, ¿habla español?*" Marisa looked back at me as she said this, her eyes shining even in the softly lit corridor.

"*Sí, pero tengo que practicar. Acabo de usar el español en mi trabajo pero ahora no.*" I felt the familiar leap my insides used to take for granted when experiencing the joy of using another language to communicate.

"*Habla bien,*" Marisa said appreciatively, which was only partly true. While I did mimic sounds well and, after many years, could pass for a comfortable speaker of Spanish, I got considerable mileage out of the shock factor. No one expects a fair-skinned Midwesterner to be able to shoot the jive in *el español*, particularly without resorting to "*¿Dónde está el baño?*" or "*Más cerveza, por favor.*"

Marisa stepped aside to allow us entrance to a room where the Zimmermans had gathered with their other guests. I smiled and waved to Kylie across the room and looked behind me to finish my conversation with Marisa, but she'd left. The kitchen door, far down the hall, was swinging in her wake.

We were one of three couples Kylie and Russ had invited to dinner. I pulled Jake in the direction of the others, though I was certain he would have been perfectly content checking out the Zimmermans' digs for the rest of the evening. We'd been led to the library. Built-in cherry bookshelves lined the walls and arched all the way up to fourteen-foot ceilings. The room had been fitted with a polished brass ladder that ran along the perimeter.

I scanned some of the titles as we walked. Lots of dark, leather-bound volumes that looked like they hadn't seen much face time. Pockets of horizontally displayed art books mingled with framed photos, small vases, and delicate ceramics. One section was tightly shelved with trade paperbacks. Judging from the scrolled script on many of the spines, I assumed this was the religious section. I made a quick scan for the Rich Jesus book, but Kylie approached before I could finish. She wore a shimmery coral number on top, which pulled to the side in a big knot. Her black formal trousers were tailored to her frame and fell gracefully around three-inch black heels.

Her embrace was conspiratorial. "Welcome," she said into my ear, as if this were the ancient password involving something that would upset the pope. She pulled away and extended her hand to Jake. "You must be Jake."

Jake grinned. "And you must be Kylie. Great to meet you."

"Jake, I have to tell you," Kylie said, shaking her head. "Your wife is amazing. We are thrilled to have her on our team."

They stood smiling at me, the brand-new puppy with a bow on top. Jake wrapped his arm around my waist. "Yeah, she's pretty great, even if she married up."

I pinched Jake in the ribs as a gentle reminder. I'd warned him earlier that these people might not be known for their comedic timing. And true to form, Kylie stood still, head tilted and smiling but without a laugh on the horizon. "Thanks for your kind words, Kylie," I said brightly. "I've been looking forward to introducing you to Jake."

"Come," she said, guiding us to the center of the room,

where Russ stood talking with the other two couples. I greeted Mallory, the no-longer-skinny pregnant lady who was accompanied by her nervous husband, Eric. The nerves could have been the result of Mallory's burgeoning belly, though she assured us she had a good three weeks to go before Eric needed to keep his cell phone handy.

"Easy for her to say," Eric mumbled, running a hand over his shaved-clean head and shifting on his feet. "She knows *she'll* make it to the delivery."

Jake caught my eye and looked away quickly, maybe hoping I wouldn't notice Mallory was pregnant and I was not. No such luck.

The other two guests were old friends of Kylie and Russ and were both Solomon's Closet consultants. Mac and Lily had met the Zimmermans in the very beginning stages of the business, nearly ten years prior, and had gotten in on the ground floor. As a result, they were rolling in it.

"Exceptional Cab," Mac said, holding up his glass of wine. "What year?"

I glanced at Jake, hoping he wouldn't make some smart comment about his favorite vintage of Bud. He seemed safe, accepting the glass of Pinot Noir his host handed him.

Russ shifted his drink to his left hand. "Jake, I'm Russ Zimmerman. Thanks for coming."

Jake put his glass down before accepting Russ's hand, which was fortuitous, as the shake was so vigorous it made Jake's fingers turn white.

"Thanks for having us," Jake said, trying to be discreet as he stretched his crushed fingers postgrip.

Kylie excused herself to check on things in the kitchen. I

turned to Mallory and Lily. "Are you getting excited?" I asked Mallory.

"Oh, yes. I really think the fall line is the best we've seen." She nodded vigorously while clutching a tumbler of water. A wedge of cucumber trembled between the ice cubes as she nodded.

It took me a moment to register where I'd gone wrong. Lily was biting her lower lip to hide a smile.

"Oh, right," I said. "I meant are you getting excited about *the baby*?"

Mallory's blue eyes got wide. She flipped back a strand of honey hair and said, "Ooooh, the baby. Yes, yes, I'm getting very excited. Sorry about that." She let out a high-pitched giggle. "Must be the hormones!"

Lily tried resurrecting the downward spiral. "I know I felt more than a little loopy with my three."

"You know what?" Mallory said, plunking down her tumbler on a nearby coaster. "I need to find the potty. This baby loves jumping on a full bladder." She waddled over to Russ, who took her arm to show her to the restroom.

I turned to Lily. "How old are your children?" I bit into a slice of bruschetta piled with ripe tomatoes, balsamic vinegar, and fresh basil. Glorious.

"All girls, all in high school. A senior, a junior, and a freshman." She raised her eyebrows and took a sip of wine. After a moment, she said what I'd been thinking. "We had them pretty close together."

"I admire you," I said. "I'm just now gathering the courage to have another, and my daughter is four."

She chuckled. "Those first few years are pretty intense."

She searched my face. "I admire *you*, lady. At least my youngest was in kindergarten by the time I started with Solomon's. How are you managing?"

I took a deep breath. "Honestly?"

She nodded. "Hit me."

"It's been a little rougher than I'd anticipated."

Lily waited, her face open.

"For example, Nora—that's my little girl—has become interested in expressive art. Yesterday she gave me a picture she drew of a woman in a billowing black dress and a little girl who was crying. She said it was an unnamed mother and daughter and that the daughter was crying because she missed her mommy."

"Ouch." Lily winced.

"Exactly." I took a sip of seltzer. "I laughed about it at the time, but it seems to sting worse the more I think about it."

A burst of back-slapping laughter rose from the group of men. I saw Kylie rush past the door in the hallway, but there was still no sign of slow-moving Mallory.

Lily watched Kylie pass and lowered her voice. "It's easy to get sucked in, isn't it?"

I stared at her and decided to play dumb. "Sucked in?"

"To this," she said, dismissing the room and its opulence with a wave of her hand. "To the business, to the idea that money makes things easier." She looked at me. Her smile was wry. "It doesn't, by the way."

I blurted before the censor kicked in, "I can't imagine Kylie saying that."

There were a lot of ways she could have gone with that statement, but Lily just shrugged and smiled. "Kylie is Kylie. This is a beautiful home, and her kids will always have enough. Too much, probably. Mine, too." She shook her head. "I've known Kylie for a long time and I've watched Solomon's Closet grow to be a fantastic business that really does help women improve their quality of life, financially and otherwise. But," and she shrugged, "it's not for everyone. And it's not for every season. You won't see that on our brochures, but that's the truth."

I could feel something stirring in my gut and I wanted to keep Lily talking, but Mallory was coming our way and Kylie had joined Russ at his side. "Friends, dinner is served."

We followed host and hostess to the dining room. Jake and I were last in the procession. "What do you think?" I asked softly, careful to make sure Mallory and Eric, ahead of us, were out of earshot.

"Russ made his first million by thirty." Jake was hissing, which was not the best way to blend in.

I elbowed him for the second time that evening. "I told you this was a whole new ball game."

"But we're not even talking baseball anymore," Jake said, trying to whisper but sounding a lot like a boy whose voice hasn't changed. "Instead of baseball, we've moved to dodge-ball. Or extreme sports, like cliff jumping or shark riding or something."

"You and I both know that shark riding is not a sport."

Jake didn't answer because he'd entered Gawk, Phase III. The dining room was gold. All gold. Gold threads in the wallpaper, gold hues in the marble floor, gold place settings, gilded gold frames around mammoth mirrors on two of the walls. It's true that the Liberace effect presented a substantial risk, but somehow they pulled the whole thing off. Dramatic splashes of color were in two tall arrangements of bright red poppies, deep purple calla lilies, and greenery, which sprang up along the centerline of the table.

We sat in our assigned seats, places marked in frilly gold lettering on heavy white paper. After we murmured our admiration of our surroundings, Russ waited in a beat of silence and then said, "Let us pray."

We bowed our heads.

"Heavenly Father," Russ said, his baritone dropping a notch into formal prayer tone, "we thank Thee."

Thee?

"We thank Thee for Thy many blessings bestowed on this family, this family in Christ."

Kylie hummed in agreement.

"You are good, dear Lord, and all the time You are good."

"Yes," Kylie said.

I peeked at Lily, who sat silent and still.

"Help us to remember the less fortunate, the poor You said would always be among us." Russ made it sound like it was their own fault, darn poor people.

"And we ask You to bless the food we are about eat. Thank You for the blessing of sharing a meal with friends."

Just as if we're around a campfire, I thought.

"In the name of Jesus I pray these things, Amen."

"Amen," we echoed, opening our eyes and letting them become accustomed again to the candlelight.

The food was phenomenal, coming from the Latin *phenom*, meaning otherworldly, unusually brilliant, make a movie out of it starring John Travolta and Kyra Sedgwick. A salad dressed with flavors that had joined in a lovely, symbiotic marriage. Soup involving just the right amount of cream. A cut of beef so tender I didn't want to know the price per pound. Steamed veggies, truffle-infused mashed potatoes, rosemary and Parmesan dinner rolls served with three kinds of whipped butter. I wanted to lick the plate but was unable to do so and still be considered socially appropriate.

The plates had been cleared and we were basking in the after-dinner glow when it all went awry. The men were talking about their golf games and I was sitting with a goofy grin on my face, happily digesting and in no hurry to move. But Kylie started fidgeting and looking past me at a door leading to the kitchen. After a few minutes, she excused herself and bolted out of her chair, nearly colliding with Marisa, who entered at that moment carrying a plate of triple-layer carrot cake in each hand.

"Not yet," Kylie said in a tone my mother would have called "snippy" if we had company and something else entirely if we'd been alone.

Marisa lowered her head and muttered an apology. Everyone else at the table was engaged in lively banter and seemed oblivious to the interaction going on near the swinging door.

Kylie wheeled Marisa around by the shoulders and whispered through clenched teeth. "Coffee first, idiot. How many times did we go over this?"

Marisa hurried out of the room. Kylie turned around and saw me staring at her. She smiled and put her hand on my shoulder as she passed. "New girl," she said with a short laugh. "Late with the coffee, but she'll be out in just a minute. Would you prefer tea, Heidi?"

I shook my head mutely and watched Kylie settle back into her upholstered chair. I spied on Marisa the rest of the evening when she came in with coffee, then cake, then to clear the dessert plates. I tried catching her eye, wishing I had a ticker tape across my forehead that could tell her in Spanish that I thought she was doing a great job and that I was appalled by Kylie's behavior. Kylie heard me say *gracias* when Marisa retrieved my coffee cup, which launched her into a discussion of her last trip to Cabo and how abominably crowded the beaches had become.

By nine thirty I was ready for my bed and our three-bedroom shanty. After dessert, Russ had led us to a sitting room adjacent to the dining hall. Jake caught my eye from his chair by a limestone fireplace. We were the first to go, but I was happy to volunteer the babysitter excuse. We bid our good-byes to the others and thanked Kylie for the evening. Russ walked with us to the front door. It had begun to rain, so Russ stood with me in the foyer while Jake went to pull up the truck.

"It was such a pleasure to meet you, Heidi," he said, standing close to me and smiling. His eyes were shining, perhaps from the bottle of Merlot he'd kept stationed at his end of the table.

"It was a lovely dinner," I said. "Your home is amazing."

Russ nodded, his eyes glued to me. "Thank you, Heidi. One sale at a time and you'll be living in Avalon before you know it."

"I can't imagine," I said, and I really couldn't. I wondered if there were rules in Avalon against watching your neighbors from your front porch. Somehow I couldn't see the Avalon

Neighborhood Association endorsing Martin Angelo's Bunsen burner experiments. "Thank you for having us," I said, seeing Jake's headlights sweep across the lawn as he turned up the drive.

"You're very welcome," he said, smiling and sizing me up. I felt rather like an item on eBay. "I always enjoy meeting Kylie's new recruits."

I'll bet, I thought, instinctively taking a step backward.

Russ made up for the distance I'd created. He leaned into my ear and draped an arm around the small of my back. The warmth from his hand seeped through the thin fabric of my dress. "You just let me know if I can do anything for you."

I twisted away and walked to the door, looking back once as I heaved it open, but Russ was already strolling back down the hall.

When I slammed the door to the truck, I was trembling.

chapter/nineteen

It must be a primal instinct in males. I used to think it was an issue of territory, kind of like a dog marking every fire hydrant on a city block. But I'd come to believe that Jake freaked out about other men noticing his wife because marriage was hard enough as it was without introducing a third person. Maybe I was giving my husband too much credit or making his reaction too cerebral, but we'd been through some hard knocks in this area, and Jake's response to Russ's advances were not polite, to say the least.

"I'm going to wring his slimy neck and use that Mafia gold chain he was wearing to do it."

I sighed. It was very late, two hours since we'd arrived back home after the Zimmermans' party. The rain that was falling when we'd left Avalon had blossomed into a full-fledged August thunderstorm and was pummeling the roof above our bedroom. We lay in the dark, staring at the ceiling, which illuminated to daylight white when lightning struck.

"I don't think neck wringing is an option."

"It absolutely freaking is."

Increasing usages of "freaking" meant we were on a slippery slope. "Jake, let's just sleep on it and talk about it in the morning." I turned onto my side and tried making my eyes stay shut.

"I mean," Jake said, propping himself up on an elbow to face me, "who *are* these people? The wife insults her maid, probably because the poor girl's not a WASP and she thinks she can get away with it, and the husband hits on my wife as soon as I'm out of earshot?" He was seething. "And he *prayed* before we ate!"

"Lots of Thees and Thous." I molded my pillow into a minimountain under my head.

"Exactly," Jake said, slapping the comforter with his hand. "Who prays like that?"

"I've heard Mormons do. As a matter of respect for the name of God. Maybe we could use more of that."

"Heidi," Jake erupted, "are you on crack? You're saying skanky Russ has more respect for God than I do?"

"That's not at all what I'm saying," I said. "Can we not get into the spiritual ramifications here?" I thought of all the pretty turquoise and brown price tags in my basement with Bible verses attached and felt sick to my stomach.

"You have to quit."

"I can't quit."

"Yes, you can." Jake pulled on my shoulder until I faced him. "Quit."

"Jake, you and I both know we need the money. Especially now, trying to get pregnant." Dr. Kahn had said we'd give it four more cycles before starting medication, which was expensive and not covered by Jake's insurance. And the longer it took, the more costly the treatment. Now was not the time to quit my job.

"We'll figure something out."

"Something that lets me still stay home with Nora and

make more than I would as a Wal-Mart greeter? I'm already doing pretty well, and if I can get some people signed up under me. . . ." I trailed off.

Jake was silent. I shut my eyes but knew he was watching me. "Your choice," he said finally, rolling onto his back.

"I'll think about it," I said. I pulled his arm around me and rested my head on his chest. "Can we sleep now?"

He kissed me on my forehead. "I love you."

"Love you, too," I said. I lifted my face and nuzzled into his neck. "Rambo."

"Watch it," he said.

We slept like that the rest of the night, arms and legs entwined but lost in separate dreams.

℮ ϑ ℮

The following Monday Nora and I stood on Willow's front step. My daughter had pushed the doorbell no fewer than five times and was hopping from one foot to the other. Visits to Willow's house were like candy for her. Our hostess treated Nora like treasured though misunderstood royalty. The two of them were in cahoots, and instead of fighting it, I'd decided long ago to let kindred spirits be kindred spirits.

Willow opened the door and Nora gasped.

"Welcome, dear sisters," Willow said in a rich alto, bowing in greeting. "Please, come into my enchanted home."

"Thank you," Nora whispered, tiptoeing under Willow's arm and into the house. This was our weekly slot when Willow and I met to talk, but I'd felt guilty calling Micah to come babysit yet again, so I'd brought Nora with me. I knew that meant our conversation would be fragmented and distracted, but Willow wasn't one for rigid rules anyway, and Nora's depressing artwork was doing a number on my guilt load.

"Nice getup," I said to Willow.

"Isn't it fabulous?" She sucked in her cheeks and puckered her lips like an extra in the "Vogue" video. She looked like an acid trip with kinky hair. She wore a flowing caftan made of purple gauzy material and embroidered with red thread. Vertical rainbow stripes ran down her pants and ended in bell-bottom cuffs with the diameters of hula hoops. She'd wrapped a beaded scarf around her head, which provided a brief break in the red curls she'd brushed out to Don King-like proportions. "Would you believe I found all of this in my own closet?"

"Shocking."

Willow narrowed her eyes at me as we stepped into the living room. Nora was already scavenging through the battered trunk Willow had lugged downstairs for the occasion. Nora loved that trunk. The contents varied according to season and Willow's whims, but it was understood that Nora had free reign to whatever she found. One especially dreary day in February, Willow had decided on a beach theme, and Nora had opened the lid to find grass skirts, sidewalk chalk, buckets and shovels, and even a Rubbermaid tub of sand. There was a brief film noir phase when all the items had needed to be either black or French or both. Nora was too young to appreciate artistic angst, it turned out, and besides, what was film noir without a good cigarette? Even Willow allowed for censorship when it came to tobacco and preschoolers. The Library trunk had been a big hit, containing fake horn-rimmed glasses, a rubber stamp and stack of sharpened pencils to help patrons with checkout, and a mountain of books Willow had chosen from her own neighborhood library. Hippie Trunk was already educing squeals of pleasure, and Nora had uncovered only a collection of Indian bangles so far.

Willow shook her rainbow booty to "Aquarius" coming from her speakers. "I knew she'd love it. This should give us at least a half hour, don't you think?"

"Thanks for letting me bring her along." I dropped in behind Willow en route to the kitchen and a fresh pot of coffee.

She waved away my thanks. "You know she's welcome anytime. I remember how hard it was to get away, even once a week."

I circled the table and sat where I could see Nora through the doorway. "I'm sorry I've been MIA."

Willow brought over two plates of warm and crumbly coffee cake. "What's with all the guilty apologies?" she asked, reaching for the coffee pot.

I inhaled the smell of Costa Rican dark roast before answering. "Sorry."

Willow raised her eyebrows over the cup that steamed in her hands.

"I mean, I'm not sorry. I just miss seeing you. Especially considering I've been in need of good counsel."

"What's going on?" Willow settled back in her chair. Her eyes were trained on my face.

"Wait," I said. "Before we get into the sordid details, how are things with David?"

She smiled. "Things are good." She shrugged and cupped her mug with both hands. "We're just enjoying each other's company. Movies, restaurants, jazz clubs. Nothing too serious and certainly no wedding bells."

I loved hearing the words *wedding bells* from a woman wearing a headband and bell-bottoms.

"But it's nice," she continued. "I don't think I'd realized how lonely I was."

"I'm happy for you," I said and squeezed her hand across the table. "And I'm even happier for David, who must be clicking his heels to have found such a catch."

"True enough. He's one lucky sap." She winked. "I'm trying to compensate for all your weird self-deprecation." Tiny wrinkles around her eyes creased into familiar position as she smiled.

How could I be anything but authentic with a face that open? "Okay," I said, taking a deep breath. "Remember Kylie? My boss?"

"Wiiiiiiiiilloooooow," Nora called. Her voice was muffled. "Can you help me?"

I looked through to the living room and saw Nora's head stuck in the bodice of a paisley-print dress with spaghetti straps and a crinkly, pleated skirt. Skinny, tanned arms flailed out of the arm holes. Willow went to help Nora dislodge. She waited while Nora did some turns on an imaginary catwalk and helped her accessorize with leather moccasins and a hemp necklace.

"Okay," Willow said as she walked back to the kitchen. "Kylie, your boss."

"Right. Kylie, my boss, has built this empire of a business out of nothing, lives in this monstrous house in Avalon, and is married to a guy named Russ. So they had us over for a dinner party—"

"Wiiiillooow," Nora called. "The music stopped."

Willow bit back a smile as she rose from the table. "I guess I was being optimistic with a whole half hour."

"I'm sorry."

"Quit that," she said over her shoulder. She reloaded the CD player with Steve Miller and returned to the kitchen. "Dinner at Avalon."

"We went to dinner at Kylie and Russ's house in Avalon. I'd had hints already that Kylie and I might have different ideas on how to treat people, but that night—"

"I have to go potty!" Nora came careening into the kitchen and nearly wiped out on the tile in her slippery moccasins.

The phone rang and Willow went to answer it as I herded Nora to the bathroom. I was helping her wash her hands at the pedestal sink when Willow poked her head into the room.

She held the phone out to me. Her hand covered the mouthpiece. "It's for you," she whispered. "She said she couldn't find your number and I said you happened to be here."

I saw a quizzical look on my face in the reflection of the bathroom mirror. I stepped out in the hall and Willow moved around me to help Nora. "Hello?"

"Heidi, hi." It was Laura Ingalls Wilder. "I'm sorry to bother you at Willow's. I'll only need a minute."

If I hadn't known better, I'd have thought she sounded *giddy*.

"Hi," I said, moving aside as Nora ran past me with Willow hot on her tail. "How are you?"

"Fine." She lowered her voice and enunciated. "Heidi, we need to talk."

Oh, dear. Upset about the Communion controversy?

Worried that I was corroding our social fabric by selling things like Hyssop and Honey Personal Lubricant? "Sure," I said, cringing.

"Can we meet at your house this afternoon?" She was whispering.

"That would be fine. Nora naps after lunch. Shall we say one thirty?"

"I'll be there." *Click.*

I couldn't picture it, but I wondered if Laura had been watching too much *24*.

"What was that all about?" Willow asked when I rejoined her and Nora by the trunk. Nora had changed into a T-shirt that had a metallic screen print of the Village People on the front. The shirt nearly fit her, which meant it'd been a bit, *ahem*, snug on Willow back in the day.

"She wants to meet at my house this afternoon."

"What about?"

I shook my head. "She didn't say. She was talking all hush-hush and paranoid. Is she into conspiracy theories or something?"

Willow became somber. "Well, I know I am. There's no way the deaths of Jack and Bobby Kennedy were unrelated, not to mention Martin on that Atlanta balcony and Marilyn Monroe's 'suicide.'" She made quotation marks with her fingers.

I waited for the punch line, but Willow only looked sad.

"And what—do you shred all your documents, too?" I snorted.

Her eyes narrowed. "Have for fifteen years. And with a particle shredder, not strips that some garbage diver could paste back together in five minutes."

I shook my head in wonder. "And you think you know a person."

Nora was shuffling around the room in a pair of white go-go boots.

"I suppose we should go," I said, looking at an oversized clock on the mantle. "I need to have Nora lunched and quarantined before the CIA Agent for Jesus arrives. Maybe she'll bring her own Breathalyzer."

"Love you, sweet girl," Willow said, her head ducked into a deep hug with my daughter.

"What do you say to Willow?" I said to Nora.

"Thank you, Willow," Nora said. "It was a lovely day spent with lovely company."

Willow stole a glance at me as she opened the door for us.

"*Alice in Wonderland*?" I said with a shrug.

"You're very welcome, Norie. Come back anytime to Willow's Shack o' Love."

Nora skipped down the front steps but Willow called after her. "Wait just a minute, missy. You didn't say a proper good-bye."

Nora turned, grinning. They faced each other and, with sober faces, locked eyes and shimmied like Steve Martin.

"Thanks, Willow," I said after their sobriety had given way to giggles. Nora was doing somersaults on the front lawn. "Maybe next week we can talk about the Kylie debacle."

She hugged me. "I'll bet you already know what to do anyway." She put both hands on my shoulders. "Do what all wise people of faith have done since the beginning: Pray about it, think about it, and then mix heart with head to make a good decision. Not forgetting, of course, that grace will catch you if you really screw up."

She smiled.

I went to unlock the car and said over my shoulder, "I'm telling on you that you said 'screw.' You are so busted."

"Go ahead," Willow said, her eyes twinkling. "But you might have better luck if you loan her my go-go boots. They always had a liberating effect on me."

I giggled while intercepting Nora midsomersault. I carried her by the ankles to the car. We pulled away, but Nora waved at Willow for two full blocks until she couldn't see the mane of curls and purple shirt even when she squinted.

chapter/twenty

"Would you like some more tea?" I asked.

Laura Ingalls shook her head and kept fiddling with her napkin. She'd been sitting at my kitchen table for almost fifteen minutes and I still didn't know why she'd come. I'd run around the house like a maniac while Nora ate her lunch, stashing anything that might be objectionable in Laura's mind. The obvious no-no's took only a minute: Our small wine rack had been relocated to the basement closet, and a lone bottle of beer now hid behind orange juice in the fridge. But as I scanned my house in the waning minutes before one thirty, I wondered if I'd done enough. What about my music collection? I assumed Laura was a praise-only kind of girl, maybe even hymns-only. Certainly Sgt. Pepper would concern her, what with "Lucy in the Sky." Not to mention Jake's vintage AC/DC and the leftovers from his glam rock phase. I could tell her he was now more apt to listen to Yanni, but would she listen?

And what about child rearing? I made a mental note concerning conversation fillers: Praise Ferber, disparage family beds. Laud boundaries, curse demand feeding. I would not mention that Nora had sucked a pacifier until she was three, and I would avoid mentioning Hillary Clinton altogether.

Now here we were, having tea, and Laura hadn't looked around once for hard evidence. Instead, I couldn't help thinking of my Southern friend, Wade, and his mother's worrying over his repeated curfew violations in high school. She always said she'd sit at the window, waiting for sign of Wade's headlights and feeling "nervous as a whore in church" until he was home safe and sound. The phrase was not a custom fit for Laura, I knew, but there ended up being similarities.

"Heidi," she finally said, smoothing her jean jumper with her hands. "I'd like to do what you do."

I looked at her blankly. "You would?" Certainly she couldn't be referring to my nagging problem with profanity.

She nodded. "I've given this a lot of thought over the last few weeks, and I'm sure. I want to sell Solomon's Closet Fine Lingerie."

She might as well have told me she was really Bono in disguise. Her hands fluttered to her tight chignon as she waited for me to respond.

"Solomon's Closet?" I asked, as if it were the first time I'd heard the words together. "Why?" In retrospect, I realize this may not have been the best sales move, but there it was.

"Well, I thought you'd ask that." Laura's posture was impeccable. "When we were at Willow's party, something *happened* to me." She took a deep breath and her eyes rolled to the back of her head.

I tried not to get nervous.

"For the first time in a long time, I felt *alive*. I felt feminine." She took a deep and shaky breath and then had out with it. "*I felt sexy.*" She shuddered.

I realized I'd been working my lower lip with my teeth.

"Yes, well," I said. I crossed my legs and shifted in my chair. "I'm glad you had such a positive experience."

She lowered her voice and shot a conspiratorial glance at Nora's closed door. "Heidi, it was more than an isolated event." She shook her head and raised her eyebrows. "My husband is *thrilled*." Her eyes were huge and seemed surprised by her own bad self.

I was starting to think I liked the repressed Laura better. "That's, um, great. But," I cleared my throat, "are you sure you want to make this, er, experience into a career?" My mind shot to an image of Laura's fully clothed pole dance at Willow's party. This woman would be dangerous in a position of influence.

"Absolutely," she said with a jump that made her tea slosh over the rim and onto her denim. She absentmindedly mopped at the spill with a napkin. "If I can share this feeling with other women like me, think of the good I could do!"

I tried not to think of it.

"What better person to sell the exceptional products from Solomon's Closet than a woman whose life and marriage have been drastically changed by them? I've already compiled a list of my ready-made *contacts*." She brought out a neatly folded paper from her dress pocket. "For example," she read, "I lead three Bible studies for women out of my home. Oh," she looked up. "You met one of the ladies. Do you remember Marilyn from that day at the noodle restaurant?"

I nodded, remembering the sickly looking woman who'd paled at the imbibing.

"There you go," Laura said triumphantly. "There's a woman right there who could use a Solomon's Closet intervention."

"I don't doubt it," I said into my mug.

She returned to her list. "So my three Bible studies, my neighborhood is full of women, none of whom I've really talked to much at this point, but I could, and there are the Strut-n-Stroll girls. Heidi," she said, her breath quickened and shallow, "I now know what Paul was trying to say when he wrote, 'It is for freedom that Christ has set us free.' I haven't felt this free, well, ever. I'm a new woman!" Her pinched face broke into a smile. The skin around her mouth seemed unaccustomed to the action; her upper lip trembled from overworking wimpy muscles.

I tossed back the rest of my tea and plunked the empty cup down on the table. "What does your husband think about this?" I'd never met Mr. Wilder but could imagine this New Laura had blindsided him even more than she had me. No one goes from calico and Rockports to lace and Lycra without at least a transition period.

Laura's eyes narrowed and mischief played on her lips. "Let's just say he's taken up whistling."

Gross.

"All right," I said. "Well, welcome to the team."

She clapped her hands once and whooped, "Yippee!" before checking herself and apologizing toward Nora's room.

We headed down to the basement office and booted up the Internet. Laura's chatter was constant; I barely got a nod in edgewise. After I walked her through the online registration and set up an appointment with her in a week to give her more details on the financial breakdown, we climbed the stairs and paused at the front door.

"Thank you so much, Heidi," she said, pumping my hand and drawing me toward her in an awkward embrace. When she pulled away, her eyes were shining with emotion. "I can't tell you how much it means that you have faith in me. I *know* I can do this." She stood tall, chin raised and ready to sing the national anthem. "I'll make you proud of me." With that, she opened the screen door and floated to her conversion van, revved the engine, and backed out of our driveway. She leaned over the passenger seat and waved madly at me for half a block.

Only when I was certain there were no Candid Cameras hidden in my shrubbery did I shut the front door.

℮ ꕀ ℮

From: anniebananie@wordlink.com
To: amorcita@springdale.net
Subject:

H-
I miss you. Where are you these days?

A

From: amorcita@springdale.net
To: anniebananie@wordlink.com
Subject: Life on other planets

A-
Orbiting and taking the occasional leisurely stroll through The Twilight Zone.

Miss you, too.

When are you coming home, anyway?

Hello to Superman.

H

℮ ♪ ℮

"I'm thinking of an animal," I said.

Nora chewed her celery stick. I could smell its cloak of peanut butter from across the table. "Polar bear?" she ventured.

"You have to ask questions." I took a bite of her snack. One of the most useful techniques under my parental belt, the game we were playing was designed to distract Nora long enough to get her to eat. Personally, I couldn't identify with needing a decoy to clean my plate, but I was willing to humor her.

Nora scrunched up her forehead in thought. "Does it have wings?"

"No."

"Does it have four legs?"

"Yes."

"Does it live in the ocean?"

"No."

The phone rang once, twice before I went to answer it. "Sorry, bug. I'll be back in one minute. Keep thinking." I reached for the receiver. "Hello?"

"Heidi, it's Kylie."

"Hi, Kylie." I took the cordless back to my seat across from Nora. "How are you?"

"Fine," she said hurriedly. "Thank you. I'm calling about

an SC event at my house this coming weekend. Will you be in town?"

"We just cancelled our cottage at The Hamptons, so yes."

Silence, and then a forced laugh. "Oh, you're kidding. Very funny."

I rolled my eyes.

Nora tapped me and whispered, "Does it have fur?"

I nodded at my daughter. "What can I do for you?" I said into the handset.

"Russ and I are giving a fall picnic for some initial contacts and a few midlevel employees."

I cringed at the thought of Russ and his party etiquette.

"Just a chance to get some of our people connected and to build interest among the curious."

"I know! A snake!" Nora's triumph was muted by a mouthful of peanut butter.

I pulled the mouthpiece away. "Nope. Snakes don't have fur or four legs." This game was known to take awhile.

"Heidi?" Kylie sounded annoyed.

"Sorry about that," I said. "Nora and I were playing a game when you called."

"Shall I call back when you're less distracted?"

I felt the hairs on the back of my neck bristle. "No, this is fine. You were saying?"

"We're having a picnic at our house and I need someone to tell her story of how she came to work for Solomon's Closet and how it's changed her life. Would you be willing to do that?"

"Mommmmmyyyy," Nora wailed as a warm-up to inconsolable weeping. She'd spilled her glass of chocolate milk all over the table, down her favorite T-shirt, and into her lap. She sat motionless, her hands hanging shoulder-height and limp. Despair clouded a face washed in tears.

I ran to the kitchen for a towel.

"Heidi, is everything all right?" Kylie asked in a voice that told me she couldn't care less.

"We're fine." My voice bordered on curt. "I'd be happy to talk to your picnic people." I started to mop up the chocolate liquid and decided to tell her about my new and promising recruit later.

"Excellent." Kylie gave me the date and time to arrive. "And feel free to bring Jake and Nora. It's a family affair." Suddenly she was on the task force for family advocacy.

"Thanks. We'll see you then."

I hung up and left the phone on the kitchen counter. I scooped chocolate-bathed Nora onto my lap and sank to the floor. "You okay, peanut?"

She nodded and sniffed. "I spilled on my Grover shirt."

We peeled off the shirt and sat looking at the blue and brown heap before us. "I can wash it."

"Good as new?"

"Good as new."

Nora let her head fall back on my shoulder. I felt her rise and fall with each breath. We sat like that for so long that I nearly fell asleep. But Nora piped up with one last guess.

"Raccoon."

"You're right," I said, "and the smartest celery-and-choco-late-covered sassafras in the universe."

I tickled her until she gasped for me to stop.

chapter/twenty-one

We pulled into Avalon Estates just after six, but there was already a menagerie of cars, SUVs, and minivans parked at the Zimmerman house. As if on cue, the rain we'd plodded through for days had lifted that morning to reveal a crisp and sunny fall day, the kind we waited for all through the humidity of August and pined for when the cold settled in November. We had to hoof it three blocks, which were long blocks in that neighborhood. By the time we ascended the circular driveway, my slip-on mules had begun their first protests of the evening.

We followed the elegantly lettered sign on the front door instructing us to proceed around the house to the back. I took stock of the Elliott family. I'd bribed Nora with bubble gum to get her to pull on green and pink striped capris and a matching top. This ensemble, in my daughter's opinion, was far inferior to the one she'd chosen, which involved a leopard-print bra she'd dragged out of the Goodwill bag. In addition to the poor taste involved with dressing one's child in lingerie for a picnic, there was the added concern that the bra was not from Solomon's Closet. But one piece of Bubble Yum later, she'd forgotten all about her complaints of injustice.

Jake wore linen pants the color of *dulce de leche* with a white linen shirt, sleeves already rolled up. His face was grave, his hands itching for a machete to tackle some of the vines on the Zimmermans' brick. Even better would be if Russ were wrapped up in the vines like a wayward Tarzan.

"This will be stretch for me, you know."

I took his arm. "I do know that. All I ask is for civility. You don't have to seek him out. You don't even have to be friendly." We watched Nora scamper ahead of us through the wrought-iron gate to the backyard. "Use Norie as an excuse to be completely antisocial. I do it all the time."

Jake shoved both hands in his pockets and trudged like a middle school boy on his way to the bathtub. "Only because I love you will I refrain from snapping his neck."

"That and the whole prison thing."

"No, only because I love you. A few years in the clink doesn't scare me." He worked to contain a small grin that spread from his eyes.

I stopped him right before we came into full view of the backyard. Nora was crouching just in front of us, trying to smash a box elder bug between two fingers.

I put both hands on his face and pulled his lips to mine. After a kiss that came close to *General Hospital* in terms of showmanship, I pulled away and said, "I love you, too. And I promise to reward you with sexual favors."

"Now, that's what I'm talking about," he said as we resumed our walk. "Finally, I get something out of this business venture of yours."

The backyard was filled with groups of people chatting and holding drinks. Most of the men were wearing some variation on the collared-shirt-and-khakis theme, though one man with wild curly hair wore jeans and sandals. The women were a bit more diverse in their picnic wear. In a preliminary sweep, I saw casual skirts and tops, lots of capris, and a few sundresses getting in their last appearances of the season. I spotted Kylie on the back patio, smiling and talking with a couple I didn't recognize. Russ stood down the hill outside a spacious gazebo. He looked up at us but I averted my eyes quickly enough to avoid eye contact.

"Shall we eat?" I asked, grabbing Nora's hand and leading my little family toward tables heaped with food. I did double duty on my plate, piling up enough food for both Nora's and my lunch. I ignored the waiflike desperate housewife in front of me who took occasional breaks from counting her lettuce leaves to steal disapproving glances at our plate. I wondered what she'd do if I plopped a nice, juicy piece of chocolate cake right in the middle of her roughage. Pass out? Call the authorities? Her asceticism only made me heap higher my scoop of potato salad.

Nora danced between me and Jake, hopping around in time to the music coming from the gazebo. A quartet of bored-looking college students in black were playing through a set of Vivaldi and Mozart. I had a sneaking suspicion this was to pay the bills and that they would have much preferred a lineup of Coldplay and Kravitz. Or at least Stravinsky.

Russ and Kylie's backyard was dotted with quilts for seating. We sought out an orange and blue blanket under a sprawling maple with leaves that had begun to turn. Our low canopy was still awash in green, but traveling upward, the color turned first to orange and then an explosive red. The quilt on which we sat spanked of that recently-shipped-from-the-Pottery-Barn-warehouse smell. I knew from a previous conversation that Kylie had an entire room devoted to entertaining, which she'd dubbed The Theme Room. After their debut today, these quilts would likely join their cousins in The Theme Room, placed in roomy containers labeled "Outdoor Picnic"— not to be confused with "Indoor Winter Picnic," designed to break up winter blues, nor "Harvest Party/Square Dance," which would be coming round the mountain in a month or so.

"The fried chicken is good," I said to Jake and Nora.

Jake nodded. His back was turned to the yard, eyes fixed on his plate.

I tried my other conversational possibility. "Do you like your lunch, Norie?"

"More cheese chunks, please." She already had her grubby hands all over a handful of Colby Jack. Here we were, lunching at one of the biggest houses in the state, and what does my daughter eat? Not foie gras. Not prosciutto-wrapped melon. Not even a thin slice of pecorino Romano, which was still cheese. No, she wanted squares of Colby Jack, just like the plastic-wrapped ones in our fridge at home.

"Nora, don't you want to try some of this croissant? It has cheese, ham, lots of good stuff." I offered it to her.

She wrinkled her nose. "Yucky." She picked over the rest of our plate and settled on a strawberry and two pieces of pineapple. Soon she jumped up and asked to go play. I fought for a few more bites and then gave up. I didn't stand a chance next to the nickel-brushed buckets of pinwheels and bubbles standing next to the patio.

Soon after Nora scampered off, Marisa approached us

carrying a tray of lemonade and iced tea. She smiled when she recognized us. *"Buenas, señora, señor. ¿Quieren algo de tomar?"*

We chatted for a while about the perfect weather, Marisa's plans to visit her family in Nicaragua over Christmas, her new apartment in downtown Springdale. Just when I was getting the courage up to ask Marisa what she thought of her employer, Kylie herself walked up and interrupted us.

"Welcome, Elliotts," she said, sitting down on the quilt and leaning over to peck me on the cheek. Marisa ducked her head and hurried away, her presence unacknowledged by Kylie. "Are you having a nice time?"

We assured her we were, though my assurances were more enthusiastic than my husband's. Jake was suddenly deeply absorbed in his glass of lemonade.

"I'd ask you to make sure you mingle with the new people, but I know you have other things on your mind," she said to me. "Are you ready to give your talk?"

I pulled an index card of notes from my pocket and waved it in the air. "Sure am. I won't take long, only five minutes or so."

"Perfect," she said, brushing off her cocoa brown prairie skirt as she rose to leave. Her feet were pedicured and tanned in strappy gold sandals. "We'll get started as soon as I can gather people up to the chairs on the patio." She walked away quickly, greeting people on her way and ushering them toward the house.

"All right, then," I said, pulling myself to my knees and getting up in stages so as not to flash the groceries at any innocent passersby. I wore a skirt as well, Nora's favorite in my wardrobe. It was deep red and full, sewn in soft layers that made it spin out when Nora asked me to test its potential.

"Let's rock this joint." Jake's face and voice were expressionless. "I'll get Nora and see you up there."

When I reached the summit of the hill behind Kylie's house, the first drops of dusk were beginning to fall on our gathering. The Zimmermans had erected a billowy turquoise and brown striped awning on their spacious patio. The chairs set up under the covering were filling up fast. I waved across the group to Lily, who was joining Mac and two of their girls in a spot near the front. I thought about making my way over to them but decided I'd be better off trying to nab three seats together on the aisle. Jake slipped into his seat just as Kylie came to stand in front of the group. Nora climbed out of his arms and into the seat between us. I got her situated with a coloring book and crayons I'd grabbed out of one of the kid buckets and tuned into Kylie.

". . . my extremely talented husband, Russ Zimmerman."

Russ joined Kylie at the front and kissed her politely. Then, winking at the audience, he spun her around and dropped her into a low dip before kissing her again. The crowd applauded and laughed appreciatively. I looked over at Jake, who sat with his arms crossed over his chest. When Kylie was restored to a standing position, Russ held her tightly around the waist and announced, "I'm telling you guys out there, this Solomon's Closet stuff is just what the doctor ordered!"

Jake shifted in his seat so his head rested in his hands.

Kylie, whose smile had never wavered throughout the whole Copacabana routine, took the floor once more. "We are so honored to have you as guests at our home. We welcome you, your families, and especially your children, the ones who benefit the most from your involvement in Solomon's Closet."

I saw one of Lily's girls lean over and whisper something in Lily's ear that made her laugh. I was in and out of the next part while Kylie told the south side of Chicago story, meeting Russ, becoming a gazillionaire for her children's sake, et cetera. I'd seen Brenna and Myles being paraded through the party earlier but they'd already disappeared into the house with their nanny.

Nora held her tongue out in concentration as she colored in a picture of David and Goliath. With only the slingshot done, she let her crayon drop and announced in full voice, "I have to go potty."

Jake looked up from his patio floor vigilance and whispered, "I'll take her."

I pulled in my legs to let them pass.

Kylie was saying, ". . . But don't take my word for it. I've asked a very special woman to tell you *her* story and give you a face to put with the amazing things Solomon's Closet can do for you. Please welcome Heidi Elliott."

I rose and walked to the front. I faced the crowd as the applause dwindled and died out. I cleared my throat. "Hello. I'm Heidi Elliott and I'm relatively new to the Solomon's Closet team."

I recognized some faces in the group from the SC meetings held at Kylie's over the last few months, but most of these people were strangers to me. I checked my card and began.

"I met Kylie in a moms' exercise group," I said. "I was the one frantically throwing crackers at my child to make it through a two-mile walk, and Kylie was the one perfectly dressed, not sweating, and pushing a sleeping infant who never cried once."

Kylie smiled politely through the chuckles from the crowd.

"My husband and I had just begun talking about opportunities for a second income as I'd left my job as a high school teacher to stay home with our daughter."

"That's my mommy!" Nora shouted from the back of the group, where she was racing to her seat post-potty trip. The group turned in their seats and smiled appreciatively at Nora, who crawled up into her seat and resumed her coloring. Jake blushed and offered a quick wave to the onlookers.

"Thank you, Nora," I said. "Kylie told me about Solomon's Closet and how I would be able to continue staying home with Nora while making extra money. She said it was a great way to provide quality products to other women and would fit into my existing schedule. It seemed like the perfect arrangement, so I signed on."

In the corner of my eye I saw movement along the side of the group. Laura Ingalls Wilder had snuck in and was settling in an empty chair in the front row beside Kylie. Kylie patted her knee. Laura smiled broadly at me and gave me a thumbs-up.

"So I signed on," I repeated, consulting my index card. My heart had started to pound and I felt a heavy weight settle into my chest. I held the card with one hand and ran the other clammy one along my skirt.

I should say here that Jesus had the tendency to get loud with me. I knew many people who referred to the "still, small voice" with which God gently impressed on them what He'd prefer to happen. I have no doubt He must have started out that way with me and I hope to come to the point where He doesn't have to use the bullhorn. Nevertheless, at that point in my life and in my speech, the divine rule of thumb appeared to be that louder was better. I'm not talking audible voice here, though I've always felt a certain closeness with Moses and the whole burning bush incident. I can appreciate needing to see flames to get the point. But even without the voice, there were times, like that afternoon on Kylie's patio, when I winced at the clarity of God's not-so-subtle nudging, this time in the form of a pounding, heavy heart and a major speech revision.

"I thought this would be a good fit, but I was dead wrong."

Kylie's head snapped to attention. I caught Jake's eye.

"Solomon's Closet in theory was a lot different from Solomon's Closet in practice. I know it works for some." I was looking at Lily and Mac. Lily had tilted her head to one side and had kindness in her eyes. She nodded at me to go on. "But it's not for me."

Kylie stood up but stayed by her chair.

"Extra cash is a good thing. Comraderie with other women is good, too. Solomon's allowed me to think outside the box I'd built for myself in my role as a stay-at-home mom, and I'm grateful for that. But I think it's dangerous to mix spirituality and salesmanship. Plus," I said, shaking my head and looking at Kylie and Russ, who'd joined her standing and had clamped a protective arm around her waist, "there's something to be said about integrity. All the pretty panties in the world won't save a marriage."

kimberly stuart

Kylie's eyes widened and Russ began walking my way.

"In conclusion," I said quickly, "I'd think very carefully about what you're getting involved in. And I'd avoid the lotions. They tend to give people hives."

Last straw. Russ looked like he was about to head butt me off his property, but I scurried out of his way and down the center aisle. I heard Laura Ingalls sniffing as I passed. Marisa was smiling at me like I'd just won *American Idol*.

Jake met me with Nora in his arms and a grin on his face. I kicked off my shoes, which were killing me at that point, and hooked them in my fingers. I took Jake's hand. Eyes on our backs and burning bushes in my heart, we walked through the gate and straight for home.

epilogue

"Sweet pea, are you sure you don't want me to help you with that?"

Through the foliage, I see Nora shake her little head no.

Jake looks at me and shrugs. We are nearly to the security checkpoint in Springdale Airport, where we will greet Annie and James. The weather forecast is dicey, but Jake has put his Internet travel skills to good use and has confirmed the on-time arrival of Continental flight 1564 from Milan with a stopover in Newark. Big snowflakes began to fall on our way to the airport, though nothing is sticking yet. The roads are damp but clear.

"This is it," Jake says. We come to a stop behind a partition where a small group has congregated. They have a look of expectancy and I feel a shiver right along with them. In addition to seeing my best friend for the first time in seven months, Thanksgiving is three days away. I am the most obnoxious holiday person I know, particularly since having Nora. Something about the uterus sharing has inspired in me a fervent desire to live, eat, and breathe the holidays and make everyone around me suffer the same fate. Nora and I have already spent three afternoons making placemats with turkeys drawn on them, arranging cornucopias for every room in the house, and learning the words to "We Gather Together." And this is just a quiet warm-up to Christmas.

"*Umph*," Nora says, plopping down on the tile floor behind the other well-wishers. She lets fall the conspicuously large bouquet of flowers she's hauled all the way from the car. Jake let Nora pick them out, and of course she beelined for a bundle that exceeds her in height and weight.

"Good job, buddy," Jake says, patting her on the head. "You're one tough cookie."

"May I have a cookie?" She looks up at me with Bambi eyes.

I shoot a look at Jake. "Since Daddy brought it up, yes." I pull a Ziploc of vanilla wafers out of my purse, armed always in the fight against The Whine.

"Sorry," Jake says, swiping one from the bag. "I forget to censor sometimes."

"You're not the only one," I say. "At least you weren't speaking under a striped awning in back of a mansion."

Jake chuckles and we munch on our wafers.

The fallout from my talk at Kylie's has been ugly. After threats to sue on grounds of slander (unfounded) and defamation (a pipe dream), the Zimmermans have tried to poison the few friends I had at SC against me. Laura Ingalls, Kylie's newest pet prodigy, still regards me with a wary eye when we see each other at church, though I think I've detected a recent change from disdain to curiosity. I predict it will only be a matter of time.

Lily called a few weeks after my little speech to see how I was doing. I assured her I was better than ever and she told me to steer clear of the Zimmermans until the dust settled. She even offered to come by to pick up my SC promotional materials belonging to the company. I had to enclose a fat check for all the sample items I used at the parties since my contract cited any products used for my profit as "used merchandise and the financial responsibility of the consultant." Jake happily signed that puppy, and I'm content to use the excess as upcoming shower gifts for Annie.

A woman with a baby in a front carrier comes to stand by us. Her straight black hair falls in front of her face as she leans down to kiss the sleeping infant on the head. I watch them, a lump rising in my throat.

"You okay?" Jake asks. He stands behind me and wraps his arms around my shoulders.

I nod, leaning back and resting my head against his chest. We've gotten the go-ahead to begin taking a fertility drug to regulate ovulation starting after Christmas. Some days I'm full of hope, believing this is merely a waiting period God is using to refine and stretch me. Other days I cry a lot, watching Nora and mourning her life as an only child. But every one of those days I think about the baby we want so badly to love and raise. I marvel that I've taken Nora for granted, that I've assumed she was the first of several Elliott kids, and especially that I've complained about sleeplessness, loss of my own time, and nights on the nursery floor. I ache for a three o'clock feeding, a warm, tiny bundle wrapped in my arms and falling asleep to the rhythm of my rocking chair.

Two women speaking rapid-fire Spanish walk by, their arms entwined and busy finishing each other's sentences. I smile and think of Marisa. In the weeks following the SC debacle, Marisa turned out to be my most loyal friend in the

Zimmerman household. She found my number (probably among pieces of charred refuse from a bonfire lit to blot me from Kylie's memory) and called one evening. Our conversation has been easy, like it is with friends who feel they've waited years to finally meet. I've taken Marisa to lunch with me and Nora, and she's visited for Saturday playdates with Nora and Marisa's nephew, Javier. As a result of all the hours we've spent together, Marisa has been instrumental in The Plan.

Things have picked up at Jake's store, and the money issue isn't the straitjacket it has been for the last few months, but my experience with Solomon's Closet uncovered parts of me that had been shelved after having Nora. So upon Marisa's return from her Christmas visit to Nicaragua, The Plan is to partner with her in setting up an ESL tutoring service out of our house. "Service," mind you, is a term loosely used, as I anticipate most of my clients will not be in the position to pay my fee of thirty dollars an hour. But we'll work something out so that clients will have the dignity and satisfaction of paying for services rendered and so I can pitch in my share to the family pot. I'm very excited to brush off the language learning side of my brain and to justify the two extra semesters it took me in college to earn the ESL certificate. Lupe, Willow's pastry chef, has already signed up, and Marisa has taken it upon herself to be my main source of PR in Springdale's growing Spanish-speaking community. I've had three new calls in the last two weeks.

The crowd at the security partition has grown to twenty or so. Nora jumps up when she hears a man nearby say, "Here they come."

"I can't see," Nora says, panicked.

Jake hoists her to his shoulders. Nora scans the passengers with the serious countenance of a ship's lookout. After a few moments she squeals, "I see her! Annie! Annie!" Nora is waving with both arms and I stand on my tiptoes to see over the people in front of me.

I see Annie, luminous and beautiful, her hair gathered into a loose ponytail at the nape of her neck. Her face is lit with a smile and she's walking as quickly as she can without running over the passengers in front of her. She's holding the hand of a tall man with skin the color of espresso and a kind smile. His eyes are playful as he glimpses Nora's theatrics.

Jake lifts Nora up and over and sets her gently on the ground. We hurry around to the side where potential security risks can finally hug and kiss passengers. Annie dodges a family of slow movers and runs to pick up Nora, twirling her around in a circle. She kisses her cheeks to the point of embarrassment and makes a great show of the forest Nora hands her. Jake shakes James' hand and I smile and reach out to shake as well, but Annie lunges for me first. We jump up and down while we hug. Then we pull away and enclose Nora and the men in our arms. We all stand there hugging, laughing, Annie and I wiping each other's tears off happy cheeks.

"Welcome home," Nora shouts to everyone within earshot. Through our huddle, I see people smiling at Nora and laughing at us, but only because they know exactly how we feel, that there's nothing like coming home.

etc.

bonus content includes:

► Reader's Guide

► Princess Survival Tips

► Heidi's Secret Weapon: Persuasive Chocolate
Lava Cakes

► About the Author

reader's guide

Heidi's Questions

1. Though sure of my decision to stay home with Nora, I found the issue of finances to be a tough one to reconcile in my new life. After being the cobreadwinner in the Elliott house for several years, it was difficult for me to feel like I wasn't contributing financially. It was even harder to have to ask Jake for money. Can you identify with feeling like a mooch in your own home? Have you ever resented your spouse for being the one to bring home all the bacon, or more of it than you do?

2. I've heard it said that if a stay-at-home mom were to be monetarily compensated for all the tasks she completes in a given day, she'd pull in around $130,000 a year. Will you personally consider running for public office and getting this one on the books? And just for the sake of dreaming, what would you do with all those Benjamins?

Jake's Questions

3. Would you be interested in two round-trip tickets to Capri, including local transportation and three nights'

lodging, for the low, low price of five ninety-nine per person?
4. Would it bother you if the package mentioned above involved transportation by burro?
5. What do you think about my wife's decision to cut her losses and opt out of Solomon's Closet?

Russ's Questions
6. Have you ever seen a man my age look so fantastic?
7. Can I have a few minutes of your time to show you how Solomon's Closet can help you live the life you've always wanted?
8. Don't I have a couple of kids around here somewhere?

Laura Ingalls Wilder's Questions
9. How do you think I'll fare as a Solomon's Closet rep? Speak the truth in love, now. I can take it.
10. After two books, don't you think I deserve a real name?

Annie's Questions
11. In your travels, have you felt proud, embarrassed, ashamed, or a mix of emotions to be representing your hometown, your region, or your country?
12. Have you had the good fortune of eating gelato? If so, know I'm giving you a high five across the printed page. If not, next year in Italia! (See Jake about hot deals.)

Nora's Questions

13. Sometimes I feel completely underappreciated as a modern-day Cinderella. Can you identify?
14. Please state your favorite accessory, providing a visual aid if possible and a trip down your own imaginary catwalk for emphasis.

Micah's Questions

15. Would you trust your son or daughter with a tongue-pierced rocker?
16. If you have not yet procured your copy of Traumatic Static's new single, please contact the shoddy author cited on the cover of this book. And mention your disappointment that TS didn't get more attention in this novel.

princess survival tips

by Nora H. Elliott

- First and foremost, never be photographed without a tiara.
- Don't believe your mother for one minute when she says lipstick is only for grown-ups.
- Plaids are at their best when paired with polka dots.
- Fur is always in, though you might consider faux if you're a fellow animal lover.
- When applying perfume, think *quantity*, not *quality*.
- If your mom starts in again with the speech that begins, "True beauty is about a girl's heart, not her clothes and makeup," smile sweetly and agree. Believe me, it's easier that way.
- And if your mom tries to give you the speech that begins, "It's more interesting to be a girl whose life doesn't revolve around waiting for a prince to show up," please refer to the tip directly above.
- Curtsy, curtsy, curtsy.
- Choose all skirts for their twirlability.
- When in doubt, more is more, and less is boring. This applies to glitter, jewelry, and heel height.

- If your mom and dad go out on a date, which
  might happen once or twice per calendar
  year, pay close attention. Your mom is your
  greatest ally and best example of how to
  look like a grown-up princess. These nights
  are great learning opportunities for the
  princess-in-training.
- Remember, you're only as regal as you think you
  are.

heidi's secret weapon: persuasive chocolate lava cakes

1 cup Ghirardelli semisweet chocolate chips
1 ½ sticks (¾ cup) unsalted butter
3 large eggs
3 large egg yolks
¼ cup sugar
1 tablespoon flour
Additional butter and sugar for greasing

Preheat oven to 425°.

Generously grease eight five-ounce porcelain ramekins with butter. Dust the inside of each dish with approximately one teaspoon of sugar.

Melt chocolate and butter in heavy saucepan over low heat.

Beat eggs, egg yolks, and sugar in a large bowl until thick and pale yellow (about six minutes).

Fold chocolate mixture into egg mixture.

Fold in flour.

Divide batter evenly among greased ramekins. Place ramekins on a cookie sheet. *(Cakes can be made one day ahead. Keep refrigerated.)* Bake about eleven minutes until edges of cakes separate from the sides of the ramekins. Surfaces will appear cracked, but centers will still move slightly when gently shaken.

Separate each cake from ramekin with a flexible spatula and invert onto a warm plate.

Serve immediately with vanilla bean ice cream and/or freshly whipped cream to anyone you wish to impress or manipulate.

Serves eight, unless one is feeling particularly selfish.

etc.

about the author

KIMBERLY STUART lives with her husband and two children in Iowa, where she writes faithfully before laundry and during nap time. For more information about Kimberly or to contact the author, please visit www.kimberlystuart.com

CHECK OUT THESE OTHER GREAT TITLES FROM THE NAVPRESS FICTION LINE!

Wishing on Dandelions

Mary DeMuth   ISBN-13: 978-1-57683-953-9
                       ISBN-10: 1-57683-953-2

Like every teenager, Natha tries to sort out the confusing layers of love—of friends, of family, of suitors, and, desperately, of God. Natha struggles to find herself before she gives in to the scared shadow of a girl.

A Quarter After Tuesday

Jo Kadlecek   ISBN-13: 978-1-60006-050-2
                       ISBN-10: 1-60006-050-1

While visiting a local senior center filled with authentic faith, religion reporter Jonna Lightfoot MacLaughlin believes she has finally found some good news. But after a resident's mysterious death, Jonna learns that someone may have dark plans for the small community.

The Restorer

Sharon Hinck   ISBN-13: 978-1-60006-131-8
                       ISBN-10: 1-60006-131-1

Meet Susan, a housewife and soccer mom whose dreams stretch far beyond her ordinary world. While studying the book of Judges, Susan longs to be a modern-day Deborah, a prophet and leader who God used to deliver the ancient nation of Israel from destruction. Susan gets her wish for adventure when she stumbles through a portal into an alternate universe and encounters a nation locked in a fierce struggle for its survival.

To order copies, visit your local Christian bookstore, call NavPress at
1-800-366-7788, or log on to www.navpress.com.
To locate a Christian bookstore near you, call 1-800-991-7747.

NAVPRESS
BRINGING TRUTH TO LIFE
www.navpress.com